FACTS AT YOUR FINGERTIPS

ANIMALS AND HUMANS

BROWN BEAR BOOKS

Published by Brown Bear Books Limited

4877 N. Circulo Bujia
Tucson, AZ 85718
USA

and

First Floor
9-17 St. Albans Place
London N1 ONX
UK
www.brownreference.com

© 2010 The Brown Reference Group Ltd

Library of Congress Cataloging-in-Publication Data

Animals and humans / edited by Sarah Eason.
    p. cm. – (Facts at your fingertips)
  Includes index.
  ISBN 978-1-936333-03-5 (lib. bdg.)
 1. Anatomy, Comparative–Juvenile literature. 2. Human anatomy–Juvenile literature. 3. Human physiology–Juvenile literature. 4. Animals–Juvenile literature. I. Eason, Sarah. II. Title. III. Series.

  QL806.5.A55 2010
  590–dc22

                                       2010015169

ISBN-13 978-1-936333-03-5

Editorial Director: Lindsey Lowe
Editor: Sarah Eason
Proofreader: Jolyon Goddard
Designer: Paul Myerscough
Design Manager: David Poole
Children's Publisher: Anne O'Daly
Production Director: Alastair Gourlay

Printed in the United States of America

Picture Credits

Abbreviations: b=bottom; c=center; t=top; l=left; r=right.

Front Cover: Shutterstock: Eric Isselee
Back Cover: Shutterstock: Sergieiev

Corbis: Charles O'Rear 40; **Photolibrary:** Animals Animals/Zigmund Leszczynski 58r, Peter Arnold Images/Kelvin Aitken 56b; **Shutterstock:** Ambient Ideas 3, 43, Yuri Arcurs 9, 57, Simone van den Berg 35, Mircea Bezergheanu 4, Ryan M. Bolton 26, Joy Brown 50, Cameilia 7, Cbpix 11, James Coleman 47, Boris Djuranovic 38, Dmitrijs Dmitrijevs 14, Peter Doomen 53, Maria Dryfhout 12, Fivespots 26, Ilya D. Gridnev 27, Iarus 46, Eric Isselée 58l, Vava Vladimir Jovanovic 25, Kletr 56t, D & K Kucharscy 59, Jesse Kunerth 37, Kurhan 16, Rich Lindie 42, Christopher Meder Photography 28, Girish Menon 18, MikeE 49, Mladen Mitrinovic 25, Christian Musat 1, 44, Nito 21, Khoroshunova Olga 22, Michael Pettigrew 51, Dr. Morley Read 57, Serhiy Shullye 40, Audrey Snider-Bell 48, Kenneth Sponsler 30, Jens Stolt 52, Tongati 54, Drazen Vukelic 6, Arnaud Weisser 46, Ludmila Yilmaz 10, Zolran 45, Zurijeta 19.

Artwork © The Brown Reference Group Ltd

The Brown Reference Group Ltd has made every effort to trace copyright holders of the pictures used in this book. Anyone having claims to ownership not identified above is invited to contact The Brown Reference Group Ltd.

CONTENTS

ANIMAL DIVERSITY

Animals occur in practically every habitat on Earth. Some filter food; others munch plants or catch other animals to survive.

Biologists divide all living things into vast groups called kingdoms. Until recently, five kingdoms of life were recognized: plants, animals, fungi, bacteria, and protists. However, many biologists now view protists as being many different groups of simple life-forms and not a kingdom as such. Animals form the kingdom Animalia. Kingdoms are divided further into large groups called phyla. Each phylum is separated into classes, then orders, families, genera, and species.

What is an animal?

Despite their tremendous diversity, all animals share a number of common features. Animals are multi-cellular organisms—they are formed of many cells that usually form a series of tissues and organs. Animal cells do not have rigid cell walls as those of plants do. Almost all animals possess a gut because they cannot make their own food, as plants can, and must eat to obtain energy. Most animals also have a nervous system that allows them to respond quickly to their environment.

Animals vary enormously in structure, feeding habits, reproduction, and behavior. Their lifestyle as adults may be free living, **sessile** (stay in one place throughout their adult lives, like corals), or parasitic (living in or on another creature). Animals may live in groups, like ants, wildebeest, and prairie dogs, or live alone, seeking a partner only for breeding, as cougars and moose do.

The invertebrate world

Most animals are **invertebrates**—they do not have a backbone. Take a look in your backyard, and you will see invertebrates all around: snails clustering at the bases of plants, earthworms in the soil, and butterflies flapping overhead. There are around 25 invertebrate phyla, including mollusks, echinoderms (starfish and relatives), and a variety of worms. The simplest invertebrates are placozoans, which consist of just a few thousand cells. Sponges are larger and contain millions of cells. Their cells carry out different functions but do not form organs. Jellyfish are more advanced. They have organs and nerve cells so they can respond to the surroundings.

Coral reefs are home to an amazing biodiversity. More than 25 percent of all the fish in the world's oceans live by coral reefs.

Some invertebrate phyla are very small. The recently discovered Cycliophora, for example, contains just a single tiny species that lives on the lips of Norway lobsters. By contrast, other phyla contain enormous numbers of species. Mollusks include animals as different as clams, slugs, and squid. The most diverse of all animal groups, though, are the arthropods. They include animals such as crabs, spiders, and centipedes, plus the largest group of all, the insects. There are at least 2 million species of insects, but there may be 10 million or more yet to be discovered.

Backboned animals

One phylum of the animal kingdom called the Chordata includes a group of animals that have a hard internal skeleton and a backbone. They are called **vertebrates**. The backbone protects the spinal cord, which carries signals between head and body. There are five main groups of vertebrates. They are

fish, amphibians, reptiles, birds, and mammals. There is an amazing variety of vertebrate shapes and sizes. Fish called dwarf gobies are just 0.3 inches (8 mm) long and weigh less than 0.04 ounces (0.1 g). By contrast, blue whales can reach 108 feet (33 m) long and weigh up to 135 tons (122 t)!

Early vertebrates were ocean dwellers. They did not have jaws. Today, just two kinds of jawless vertebrates remain, hagfish and lampreys. Lampreys attach to larger fish, gouge a hole with their teeth, and drink their blood.

Fish and amphibians

Vertebrates include three main fish groups—sharks, ray-finned fish, and lobe-finned fish. Shark skeletons are made of cartilage rather than bone. Ray-finned fish include the largest vertebrate group, the bony fish, with more than 27,000 species. Lobe-finned fish include just the lungfish and coelacanths, but their ancestors were the first vertebrates to move onto land

---

TYPES OF SYMMETRY

Most animals are symmetrical. Their body parts match in size, shape, and position on either side of an imaginary line running through an animal. There are two main types of symmetry in animals. Most, including worms, fish, and humans, are bilaterally symmetrical. An imaginary line running down the middle of a person's body divides two

halves that are mirror images of each other. Animals such as starfish and jellyfish are different. They have a central axis around which body parts radiate. This is called radial symmetry. A few animals, such as sponges, are not symmetrical at all and take an irregular shape.

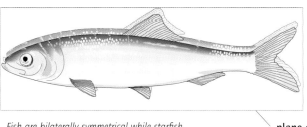

Fish are bilaterally symmetrical while starfish are radially symmetrical.

plane of symmetry

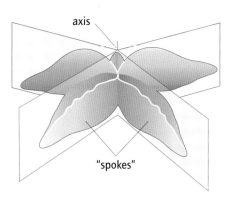

axis

"spokes"

The forelimbs of birds, such as this herring gull, have evolved into wings used for powered flight.

WHY ARE THERE NO GIANT INSECTS ?

In terms of numbers insects are the most successful group in the history of life on Earth. However, even the largest insects are no bigger than around 6 inches (15 cm) long. Biologists think that is because of the way they breathe. Insects do not have lungs as people do; instead, they have a system of tubes called tracheae. The tracheae carry oxygen from the air to every cell in their bodies. This system becomes inefficient in larger animals, placing a size limit on these creatures. However, in the past there was more oxygen in the atmosphere. Three hundred million years ago giant invertebrates thrived. They included a scorpion 2.5 feet (76 cm) long, a 20-inch-(50-cm) long spider, and a giant dragonfly with a 2-foot (60-cm) wingspan.

from the sea around 375 million years ago. Those ancient lobe-finned fish gradually evolved into amphibians, which today include animals such as salamanders, frogs, and toads. Amphibians have moist skins that soon dry out, so they usually live close to water, and their eggs need to be laid in water.

Reptiles

Reptiles evolved from amphibians. Reptiles have shelled eggs and tough, waterproof skins that allow them to range far from water. Crocodiles are the largest living reptiles; the estuarine crocodile can reach almost 23 feet (7 m) long and weighs more than a ton (1 t).

Crocodiles lay eggs in nests on land. By contrast, some lizards and snakes give birth to live young. Snakes are one of the most recent reptile groups to evolve. Boas and pythons kill **prey** by wrapping around it to constrict its breathing. Other snakes, such as rattlesnakes, inject **venom** through their hollow fangs to kill their prey.

Birds

All reptiles, amphibians, fish, and invertebrates are cold-blooded—the temperature of their bodies depends on that of their surroundings. Birds are warm-blooded and can maintain their own body temperature. Around 170 million years ago birds evolved from reptiles called dinosaurs, which may also have been warm-blooded.

Birds have feathers that help them retain heat. Their front legs form wings used for flight. Birds must be light, so they have hollow bones and lay eggs instead of carrying young inside their bodies. Birds also have air sacs in their bodies to increase airflow to the lungs and a strong heart to keep cells supplied with oxygen-rich blood.

Mammals

Birds are not the only group of warm-blooded animals to have evolved from reptiles. Mammals evolved from

Ring-tailed lemurs are mammals that live on the island of Madagascar in the Indian Ocean. Like all mammals, lemurs have a coat of fur and the mothers feed their young with milk produced by their mammary glands.

a different reptile group, the therapsids. There are about 5,000 species of mammals today, including kangaroos, mice, humans, and our closest relatives, apes and monkeys. Rather than feathers, mammals have hair that saves body heat. Two species, the platypus and the echidna, lay eggs, but all other mammals give birth to live young. Female mammals nurse their young and by feeding them with milk.

SCIENCE WORDS

- **habitat** The type of place in which an organism lives.
- **invertebrate** Animal that does not have a backbone.
- **prey** Animal caught and eaten by another animal.
- **sessile** Animal that does not move during its adult life.
- **venom** A poison delivered by a predatory animal to immobilize prey.
- **vertebrate** Animal that has a backbone.

HUMAN BODY SYSTEMS

The human body is made up of interconnected groups of organs and tissues that keep you alive, healthy, and working correctly. They are called the body's systems.

The human body's systems begin to develop very early in life. An unborn baby starts off as just a single cell—an egg cell fertilized by a sperm. This cell, or zygote, splits into two identical cells. These two cells each divide again to make four cells, and then they divide to make eight cells, and so on over and over again.

At first all the new cells are identical, but soon different kinds of cells start to appear. These cells form themselves into different types of tissues, which then develop into bone, muscle, and organs such as the heart and liver. The tissues and organs make up the basic parts of the body's systems. For example, organs such as the stomach and gut are part of the digestive system.

Major and minor systems

There are 10 systems in the human body. Six of them are called the major systems—not because they are more important than the others but because they

---

THE HUMAN BODY

This illustration shows all the major organs and systems of the human body.

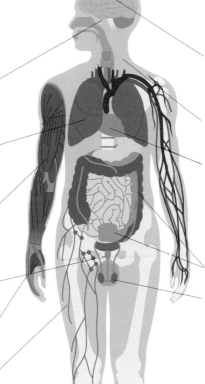

Endocrine system produces hormones (tiny "messenger" proteins) and includes the pituitary gland.

Lungs are the key organs in the respiratory system, which exchanges the waste gas carbon dioxide for the vital gas oxygen.

Muscles in the muscular system contract or relax so the body can move.

Urinary system expels fluid waste and includes the kidneys and bladder.

Tendons connect muscles to bones.

Lymphatic and immune systems are made up of lymph vessels, lymph nodes, and white blood cells which protect the body from disease.

Brain controls the nervous system, which includes nerves and the spinal cord.

Skin, hair, and nails make up the integumentary system.

Heart and blood vessels form the circulatory system, which carries gases and nutrients around the body.

Stomach, liver, and intestines belong to the digestive system, which breaks down food.

Reproductive organs enable people to produce offspring.

Skeletal system is made up of bones that protect the organs and support the body.

HOMEOSTASIS

As well as doing their own jobs, systems work together to control the physical and chemical conditions inside the body. This process, called homeostasis, includes keeping the body at the correct temperature, around 98.6°F (37.0°C). Sweating cools the body, and shivering is a warming mechanism. Other organs involved include the liver and pancreas, which control the concentration of sugar in the blood, and the kidneys, which control the body's water and salt content.

People sweat when they exercise. This helps them cool down.

extend through the whole body. The major systems are the skeletal system, the muscular system, the circulatory system (the heart and blood vessels), the nervous system (the brain, spinal cord, and nerves), the integumentary system (the skin, hair, nails, and sweat glands) and the immune system (the cells in the blood that fight infection).

SECRETS OF THE STOMACH

In 1822 a French-Canadian named Alexis St. Martin (1794-1880) was shot in the side, and the U.S. Army surgeon William Beaumont (1785-1853) treated him. The wound healed, but it left St. Martin with a permanent hole in his side that connected directly to his stomach. Beaumont realized that this was a chance to study how the stomach digests food. He tied pieces of meat, bread, and cabbage to the ends of silk strings and put them into St. Martin's stomach. A few hours later he pulled them out to see what had happened to them. In 1833, Beaumont published a description of how digestion works in the stomach.

The other four systems—called the minor systems—are mostly inside the main body cavity, the chest and abdomen. The digestive system includes the mouth, stomach, liver, and intestines. It converts food into energy and nutrients such as amino acids and sugars. The main part of the respiratory system is the lungs, which absorb oxygen from the air when you breathe in and expel carbon dioxide gas when you breathe out. The excretory system includes the kidneys; the reproductive system includes the reproductive organs; and the **endocrine system** produces **hormones** (chemicals that help control all the other systems). Some organs are part of more than one of the body's systems. The pancreas, for example, is part of the digestive and endocrine systems.

SCIENCE WORDS

- **endocrine system** System of glands that release hormones.
- **hormone** Chemical messenger that regulates life processes inside the body.

FEEDING IN ANIMALS

All animals need energy for fuel and nutrients to build and repair their bodies. They get these vital raw materials from their food.

The millions of species of animals can be divided by the different ways they feed. **Carnivores**, like sharks, spiders, and wolves, eat other animals, while **herbivores** such as cows and rabbits eat plants. Herbivores may eat a wide range of plant foods or specialize in just one. Koalas, for example, feed only on eucalyptus leaves.

Biologists call animals that eat both plant and animal foods **omnivores**. They include foxes, raccoons, and people. Other animals called **filter feeders** sieve tiny plants and animals from water, while **detritivores** feed on dead and decaying matter.

Plant food is often easy to gather, but it is less nourishing than meat. Animals that eat leaves may have to spend many hours feeding. Koalas, for example, feed for up to 18 hours each day. Other plant foods, such as nuts, seeds, and fruits, are more nourishing. Mice and squirrels hoard such foods for times when food is scarce.

Filter feeders also spend much of their time eating. Prey is difficult to find and catch, but it is nourishing, so carnivores can survive for longer between meals.

Feeding adaptations

Over long periods of time animals have evolved many features that help them feed. These are called adaptations. Herbivores, for example, have mouthparts and digestive systems that have evolved to cope with tough plant food. Water animals that eat algae, such as limpets and parrotfish, have rasping mouthparts with which they scrape their food off rocks. Mammals that eat plants have flat-topped teeth for grinding, and some, such as cows, have stomachs with many chambers to help them digest food efficiently.

A spotted hyena picks at the rotting carcass of an oryx. Hyenas usually scavenge the remains of dead animals, but packs hunt young or weak animals, including wildebeest and zebras.

Gray reef sharks are deadly predators that feed on bony fish and invertebrates such as octopuses and squid.

Plant-eaters as diverse as antelope, sheep, and termites have tiny microorganisms in their guts. They help break down a tough material called **cellulose**, which occurs in plant leaves and stems.

The bodies of carnivores are also suited to their feeding habits. Predatory (hunting) mammals such as lions and hyenas have powerful jaws and jagged teeth that grip and slice their food into chunks that can be swallowed. Birds such as eagles and falcons have sharp claws to grip prey and powerful hooked beaks to rip it to pieces.

Sight and sound

Predators rely on their sharp senses to track down their food. Herbivores also need a keen awareness of their surroundings to stay one step ahead of predators. Animals possess the same range of senses that people have. They are sight, smell, hearing, taste, and touch.

For people sight is the most important sense, yet hunters such as hawks have much keener vision. Wolves and sharks rely more on smell—detection of chemicals—when tracking down prey. Predators such as owls can hear very faint sounds that our ears cannot detect. For many animals vision is of little use for finding food at night. Small bats use sound instead. This is called echolocation. The bats produce high-pitched squeaks that bounce off objects such as moths. The bat listens for the echoes to pinpoint the prey. Most larger bats called fruit bats do not echolocate. They rely on smell and enormous eyes to find fruit to eat.

SINK OR SWIM

Many animals live and feed within the guts of people. These parasites must avoid being washed out of the body with food. Tapeworms (below) wedge their spiny head (scolex) into the gut wall. Giant nematodes do not anchor themselves, but instead swim against the tide of food—they may swim up as far as the throat.

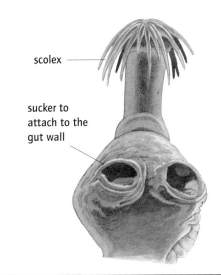

scolex

sucker to attach to the gut wall

Scents and vibrations

Your dog knows your neighborhood in a different way than you do. Humans rely on familiar sights to find their way. Your dog follows a familiar pattern of smells instead.

Smells are also important for other hunting animals. A snake gathers chemicals from the air with its flicking tongue. The chemicals are passed to a sensitive organ in the roof of the snake's mouth. Snakes use sound, too. They lack ears, but sound vibrations traveling through the ground make a tiny bone move so the snake can still detect the sounds. Scorpions also track prey by detecting vibrations; their sensors are on their feet. Fish sense vibrations in water using a sensory strip running down their bodies called a lateral line.

Super senses

Some animals possess "super senses" that humans lack. For example, snakes can detect the body heat of prey such as mice using sensitive pits in their cheeks. That allows snakes to hunt at night. In the oceans sharks and eels track prey using electric fields. Animals such as whales, bees, pigeons, and turtles can sense Earth's magnetic field. That helps them find their way as they travel over long distances.

Killing prey

Once a victim has been found, predators need a way to subdue and kill it. Many use sharp teeth and claws, but some small predators use venom instead. Jellyfish, sea anemones, and corals have tentacles with stinging cells that they use to paralyze small animals. Spiders and centipedes bite their prey and inject venom through their fangs. Snakes such as cobras use venoms that are powerful enough to kill a person, while wasps and scorpions paralyze their prey using venomous stingers on their tails.

Prey animals have a range of defenses against enemies, but some hunters have learned to overcome them. For example, a snail's shell protects it against most enemies, but thrushes are able to smash snails against stones to get at the soft-bodied creatures inside. Porcupines are covered with prickly quills that deter most predators. However, carnivorous mammals called fishers can defeat them by attacking their heads, which have few quills. Similarly, some mice can overcome the lethal chemical jets released by bombardier beetles by plunging the beetles tail-first into mud.

Hunting techniques

In the natural world predators use a variety of techniques to capture their victims. Top predators such as lions, falcons, and crocodiles mainly ambush their prey. Cheetahs quietly stalk prey such as

Rattlesnakes are highly efficient predators that subdue their prey with a venomous bite before swallowing them whole.

TRY THIS

Discover Detritivores

Soil-dwelling organisms such as mites, millipedes, and earthworms play a vital role in recycling nutrients. They are detritivores, which feed on dung and decaying plant and animal matter. To study these animals, try making this simple piece of equipment: Cut the bottom from a plastic pot, and replace it with some fine wire mesh. Put the pot into a funnel, and put some decaying leaves and topsoil onto the mesh. Put the funnel in a jar containing water, and direct a strong light onto the soil. The animals in the soil will move away from the light and drop into the jar. You will need a magnifying glass to see the detritivores.

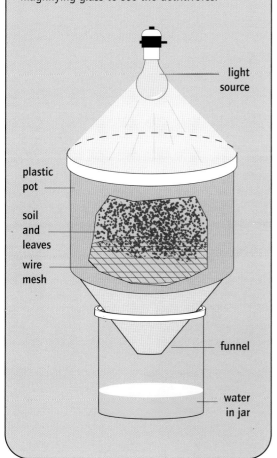

gazelles to get within range before attacking. They mainly target young, sickly, or old animals since they are the easiest victims to catch. Even so, cheetahs are often unsuccessful in their attacks.

Wolves and African hunting dogs do things differently. They work in groups to chase prey down slowly—these animals can pursue their quarry over any terrain for many hours until it tires.

Smaller predators usually rely on stealth rather than speed to capture their prey. They may simply lie in wait for passing animals. Some, such as frogs and chameleons, grab insect prey using their very long, very sticky tongues. Trapdoor spiders dash out of their burrows to grab insects, detecting them through an intricate network of silken trip wires around the entrance.

Other small hunters set traps, pits, or snares for their victims. Ant lions dig pits in sand and wait for smaller insects to fall in, while orb-web spiders weave silken snares to catch flying insects.

Anglerfish are predators with an amazing hunting aid. They attract small fish using a built-in lure. It is a long spine with a fleshy lobe on the end that looks like a worm. This tasty-looking bait dangles in front of the angler's jaws. When a fish comes close to nibble the "worm," the anglerfish pounces.

SCIENCE WORDS

- **carnivore** Animal that catches other animals for food.
- **cellulose** Chemical that forms tough molecules in the walls of plant cells.
- **detritivore** Animal that feeds on dead animal or plant material.
- **filter feeder** Animal that sieves fine particles from water for food.
- **herbivore** Animal that feeds on plants.
- **omnivore** Animal that eats both plant and animal matter.

HUMAN DIGESTION AND EXCRETION

During **digestion** the body breaks down food into tiny particles that can dissolve in the blood. The particles are absorbed and carried to the body tissues. Excretion is the process by which the body gets rid of waste products after digestion.

Your body can use the food you eat only when the food is broken down into small, simple units, or molecules. Most food is composed of long chains of molecules. The digestive system has to break the links in the chains. This process reduces the large molecules to smaller ones, which are carried by the blood to the body's cells. The cells use them as fuel or reassemble them into new chains, forming the building blocks for new tissues. The chemical reactions inside the cells produce lots of waste products, which the blood carries away. Wastes are

ENZYMES

Enzymes are proteins that speed up chemical reactions in the body. Cells contain thousands of different types of enzymes, each of which controls a particular reaction. Digestive enzymes work outside cells, inside the organs of the digestive system. They speed up a chemical reaction called hydrolysis, in which water molecules attack chain molecules and break apart the links. Digestive enzymes are produced in the mouth, stomach, small intestine, and pancreas. Examples of digestive enzymes are the proteases, which break down proteins into amino acids.

removed from the body by organs in the excretory system, such as the kidneys, and by the liver.

Digestion

Food is detected and analyzed by sense organs before and after it enters the mouth. There the food is chewed, and saliva begins to break it down. The food then passes through a long tube, called the digestive tract. In this tract chemicals called enzymes attack the food and break it down further. The

Convenience foods, such as pizza, are often high in fat. A well-balanced diet contains all the important food types, including carbohydrates, protein, and only a small amount of fat.

THE HUMAN DIGESTIVE SYSTEM

This illustration shows the main parts of the human digestive system. The sections of the small intestine absorb food and further break down the food. The large intestine is mainly important for retrieving water from the remnants of the food. The lining of the stomach and intestines would be digested themselves if they were not well protected. Glands protect them by producing a thick fluid called **mucus**, which also helps the food to move along the digestive tract.

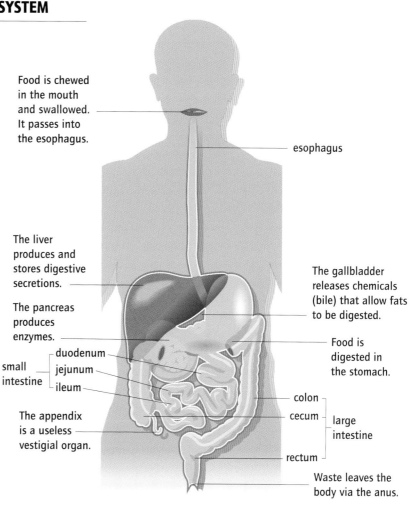

Food is chewed in the mouth and swallowed. It passes into the esophagus.

esophagus

The liver produces and stores digestive secretions.

The pancreas produces enzymes.

small intestine — duodenum / jejunum / ileum

The appendix is a useless vestigial organ.

The gallbladder releases chemicals (bile) that allow fats to be digested.

Food is digested in the stomach.

colon

cecum — large intestine

rectum

Waste leaves the body via the anus.

remains of food that have not been digested finally leave the body through an opening called the anus.

The mouth

The process of digestion begins before you even eat anything. The sight and smell of food trigger the release of a slimy fluid called saliva, which moistens the food once it is in the mouth, making it easier to chew and swallow. The saliva also contains an enzyme that begins to break down a type of **carbohydrate** in the food called starch.

The powerful muscles of the jaw work together with the teeth to cut and mash the food until it is soft and moist enough to swallow. Taste buds on the tongue detect the four main tastes in food—salty, bitter, sweet, and acidic. Gases released by the warm food travel into the nose, where their smell contributes to the flavor. When you swallow your food, it travels down a tube called the esophagus to the stomach. The food does not simply fall into the stomach. It is pushed along the esophagus by waves of muscular squeezing (contraction) called **peristalsis**.

The stomach

The stomach is a stretchy muscular bag that expands as it fills up. Food spends up to four hours in the stomach being churned around by contractions of the muscles in the stomach wall. The lining of the stomach produces a digestive liquid called gastric juice. It contains an enzyme called **pepsin**, which breaks down proteins in food, as well as hydrochloric acid, which kills germs and helps pepsin work by attacking proteins.

The stomach reduces the food to a creamy liquid, and contractions then squirt the fluid out of an opening called the pyloric sphincter into the first part of the small intestine, called the duodenum. Sphincters are rings of muscle that can open and close.

The small intestine

Most digestion takes place in the small intestine. In the duodenum food from the stomach mixes with two digestive juices—**bile** from the liver and

TEETH

People have 32 teeth, of which there are four different types: incisors at the front for cutting, canines for piercing, and premolars and molars at the back for cutting and grinding. The white, visible part of a tooth is called the crown. It is covered with a substance called enamel, which is the hardest material in the human body. Under the enamel is a hard layer of dentine, and under it is the pulp cavity, which contains blood vessels and nerves. Each tooth is anchored into the jawbone by roots.

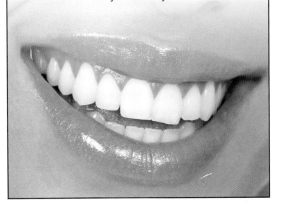

pancreatic juice from the pancreas. Bile helps the digestion of fats by making larger droplets of liquid fat break down into microscopic droplets. This process is called emulsification. Bile is stored in a small sac called the gallbladder. Pancreatic juice contains many enzymes that digest proteins, carbohydrates, and fats. These enzymes continue working throughout the small intestine.

As a meal travels along the small intestine, most of the food within it is digested into small molecules. These molecules then pass across the lining of the intestine and enter the bloodstream to be carried away to the body's cells. The small intestine's lining has many fingerlike folds called villi (singular, villus) over its surface. They are covered by even tinier projections called microvilli. Inside each villus is a network of blood vessels (capillaries) with very thin walls, which pick up small molecules from digested food.

The large intestine

Undigested food enters the large intestine, which absorbs water and leaves behind a semisolid material. Harmless bacteria feed on this waste matter. They break down some of the fiber, releasing sugar and some vitamins, which are then absorbed by the body. The bacteria also produce hydrogen, methane, and carbon dioxide gas, which can build up and cause wind.

Waste matter spends up to two days in the large intestine. It collects as a material called feces in a part of the digestive tract called the rectum. The feces are pushed out by muscles in the rectum.

The liver

The bloodstream carries digested food away from the intestines and to an organ called the liver. The liver works like a chemical factory. It carries out hundreds of tasks that keep the concentrations of sugar, amino acids, and various other chemicals in the blood just right. Excess food and iron are removed and stored in

THE HUMAN LIVER

The liver produces a bitter, dark-green or yellow substance called bile to help break down fats. The gallbladder stores the bile and releases it into the digestive system when we eat.

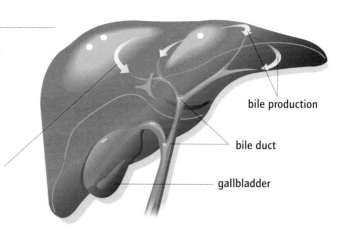

Bile is produced in the liver and enters the bile duct.

bile production

bile duct

gallbladder

the liver for later. A sugar called glucose is turned into a carbohydrate called glycogen, which can be quickly broken down and released again as glucose when it is needed in the body.

The liver also destroys poisons, such as alcohol, that enter the body with food. The liver manufactures vitamin A, breaks down worn-out blood cells, and creates bile.

The kidneys

The kidneys are two organs in the lower back shaped like large beans. They are the main organs of excretion. They continually filter the blood, removing water and chemical wastes. Each kidney contains about one million individual tubes called **nephrons**.

Blood enters each nephron through a knot of tiny blood vessels called a glomerulus. The glomerulus works just like a sieve. It allows water and other small molecules (including salts, sugars, and chemical wastes such as urea) to leave the blood and enter a long, looped tube called a renal tubule. The renal tubule is surrounded by even more tiny blood vessels. As the filtered blood moves through the renal tubule, sugars and salts are taken back into the blood, along with water. At the same time, waste molecules are left in the nephron or secreted into it.

More than 99 percent of the fluid entering the nephron from the blood is taken back into the body. The rest drains out of the nephrons through collecting ducts. It leaves the kidneys and passes along tubes called ureters to collect in the bladder. At this point the fluid is called urine. When the bladder fills up, it sends a nerve signal to the brain, causing the feeling of wanting to urinate (pass water).

SCIENCE WORDS

- **bile** A yellow fluid secreted by the liver; in the intestine it helps in the emulsification and absorption of fats.
- **carbohydrates** Sugar molecules important in respiration.
- **digestion** The breakdown by enzymes of food into small, easily absorbed molecules in the stomach.
- **enzyme** Protein that speeds up chemical reactions in organisms.
- **nephron** An excretory unit of the kidney.
- **pepsin** Enzyme in the stomach that breaks down proteins into polypeptides.
- **peristalsis** Waves of muscular contraction that ripple along the walls of the digestive system to keep food moving.

The circulatory system is all the tubes and channels (blood vessels) through which blood flows and the heart, which pumps blood around the body.

The blood vessel system is like a many-branched vine. The largest blood vessels enter and leave the heart. They get smaller and smaller as they branch out to reach all the body cells. The blood and circulatory system are essential in transporting oxygen, nutrients, and waste materials around the body. The system also helps coordinate all the other body systems. The blood is also part of the immune (defense) system. It contains white blood cells that help fight infection by microorganisms.

The heart

The heart is the engine of the circulatory system, which supplies all parts of your body with blood. The heart is a pump located in the center of your chest.

A surgeon performs a heart transplant. During the operation, the surgeon connects the patient to a heart-bypass machine, which adds oxygen to the blood and pumps it around the body while the new heart is being attached.

It has four hollow chambers; the top two are called atria (singular, **atrium**), and the two at the bottom are called ventricles. The heart's structure and function are so unique that many of its workings are still not well understood.

The tissue that makes up the heart is called cardiac muscle. Like the smooth muscle that surrounds hollow organs, such as the intestines, cardiac muscle can squeeze (contract) involuntarily— you do not have to "tell" your heart muscle to work; it does it automatically. Yet, like the muscles attached to your bones (skeletal muscles), heart muscle is striated (made of long fibers). So, cardiac muscle is a cross between smooth muscle and skeletal muscle.

Cardiac muscle also has unique connections between its cells that help all the heart's muscle cells contract rapidly and at the same time.

On average, the adult heart beats around 72 times per minute. Around 3 fluid ounces (80 ml) of blood are pumped into the main artery with each beat, so the heart usually pumps up to 11.5 gallons (7 l) of blood per minute. During strenuous exercise such as running, that can rise to 6 gallons (27 l) per minute in an average adult.

Heart control

Perhaps the most amazing feature of the heart is that it can control some of its own actions without any outside regulation, even from the brain. Tiny electrical impulses or bursts regulate the pumping of various parts of the heart. These impulses come from areas within the heart called nodes.

The sinoatrial (SA) node is located on the wall of the right atrium. The impules sent from the SA node regulate the heartbeat. So the SA node is called the heart's pacemaker. Another node, called the atrioventricular (AV) node, slows the SA node impulses to allow the atria to finish contracting before the ventricles begin contracting. The impulses are sent rapidly to cardiac cells in the ventricles through cardiac muscle strands called Purkinje fibers.

HEART DISEASE

Heart disease is one of the leading causes of death in the United States. One major cause of heart disease is atherosclerosis. This condition is the accumulation in the arteries of fatty deposits rich in cholesterol. Fatty meat is by far the food that contributes most to atherosclerosis. Some people have suggested that the government put a tax on meat to discourage people from eating it. Like the tax on tobacco, this fee could improve the health of millions of Americans and encourage them to eat more healthful whole grains instead of animal fat. What do you think of this suggestion?

Blood circulation

Blood vessels carry blood to nearly all the cells in the body. The **aorta** and other blood vessels attached directly to the heart are the body's largest blood vessels. The next largest are the major arteries, which branch into various parts of the body. Smaller blood vessels, called arterioles, branch off the arteries and get smaller and smaller, eventually forming a web of minute tubes that carry blood to every body cell. These smallest blood vessels are called **capillaries**, which are tubes with walls only one-cell thick. A mass of capillaries in a piece of tissue is called a capillary bed.

Oxygen in the blood moves from the capillaries into the cells. In return the cells release carbon dioxide as waste into the capillaries. This process, called gas exchange, occurs at the capillary bed. The capillaries that receive carbon dioxide are the beginning of the system of veins that carries oxygen-poor blood back to the heart. Like the arteries, as veins approach the heart, they become larger. The vena cavae (singular, vena cava) are the largest veins. Veins are lined with one-way flap valves that keep the blood moving toward the heart, which is why blood does not gather in your feet.

Poor diet is one of the major causes of heart disease. People should eat a range of healthy foods and avoid too much fat to stay healthy.

The smooth muscles of the arteries near where they join with the capillaries expand or contract to regulate blood flow to different areas of the body. After you eat, arterioles carrying blood to the capillary beds of the stomach and intestines open to allow more blood to flow to the digestive tract. Arterioles in the arms and legs may contract and restrict blood flow during digestion.

HEART TRANSPLANTS

Some people with diseased hearts can be saved by transplanting a healthy heart into their body. There are not enough human hearts available, however. This has led surgeons to experiment with implanting baboon hearts into people. Many people are worried by such procedures; what if baboon viruses or other diseases are passed on to humans? Some people believe that transplanting organs from one species to another raises questions about what it means to be human. Are you still human if one of your vital organs is nonhuman? Others suggest that breeding animals to kill them for their organs is wrong. Supporters say that such experiments may save many lives. What do you think?

BLOOD FLOW THROUGH THE HEART

Blood enters both atria at almost the same time from large blood vessels. They are the *vena cavae*, which carry oxygen-poor, or deoxygenated, blood from the body, and the pulmonary blood vessels, which carry oxygen-rich, or oxygenated, blood from the lungs back to the heart. Oxygen-poor blood enters the right atrium. Oxygen-rich blood from the lungs enters the left atrium.

The atria contract to pump the blood into the ventricles. When blood enters the atria, the ventricles are empty. The thick, muscular walls of the ventricles relax, increasing their volume and pulling in blood through the atria from the **veins**. The atria then contract to pump the ventricles full of blood. Both ventricles then contract forcefully. The right ventricle pumps blood into arteries that carry it to the lungs to pick up oxygen. At the same time, the left ventricle pumps its oxygen-rich blood into the aorta—a large blood vessel that channels the blood to the brain and the rest of the body.

Valves between the heart chambers keep the blood flowing in the correct direction. The veins also have one-way valves that allow blood to flow only toward the heart.

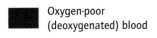

Oxygen-poor
(deoxygenated) blood

Oxygen-rich
(oxygenated) blood

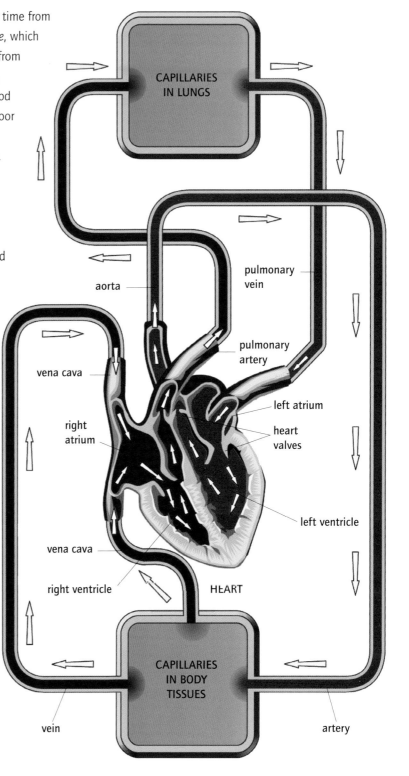

CAPILLARIES
IN LUNGS

pulmonary
vein

aorta

pulmonary
artery

vena cava

left atrium

right
atrium

heart
valves

left ventricle

vena cava

right ventricle

HEART

CAPILLARIES
IN BODY
TISSUES

vein

artery

TRY THIS

Checking Your Pulse

To check how fast your heart is beating, ask a partner to put two fingers on your wrist artery to feel your pulse. It is on the inside of your wrist. Use a stopwatch to count the number of pulses in 15 seconds. First, take your pulse when you are sitting and resting. Then, run for two minutes. Immediately after, take your pulse for 15 seconds. Multiply each number by 4 to get the number of pulses per minute. How much faster was your heart beating after you ran than when you were resting?

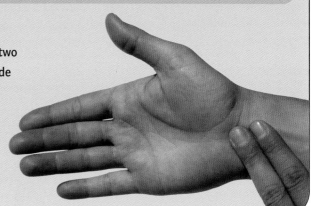

The blood

The blood carries oxygen and nutrients to all body cells and removes wastes from them. There are many types of blood cells, each with a distinct job to do. The clear liquid that carries all the blood cells is called plasma. There is about 1 gallon (5 l) of blood in an adult's body. Red blood cells contain a substance called **hemoglobin**, which transports oxygen around the body. Around 45 percent of blood consists of red blood cells. The blood cells are constantly produced in a tissue called bone marrow in the bones. An adult has around 25 trillion disk-shaped red blood cells in the blood.

White blood cells, also made in the bone marrow, are part of your immune system. They include macrophages, T cells, B cells, natural killer cells, and neutrophils. Platelets are fragments of blood cells that stick together to form a mesh of fibers, which traps more blood cells. This process results in a clot that seals an injury or wound.

DONATING BLOOD

Victims of car accidents, people undergoing surgery, and those with certain diseases such as hemophilia (a blood-clotting disorder) often need to receive blood donated by others. Each year about 4 million Americans receive donated blood. A donor's blood is tested to make sure it is healthy. Then about 1 pint (0.5 l) of blood is taken from the large vein in the donor's arm. In many cases the donated blood is then separated into its component parts, such as plasma, **platelets**, and so on. Different patients get just the blood components they need.

SCIENCE WORDS

- **aorta** Major artery leading directly from the heart.
- **atrium** One of a pair of heart chambers that receives blood before pumping it into a ventricle.
- **capillaries** Tiny, thin-walled blood vessels through which oxygen and nutrients pass into cells, with waste going the other way.
- **hemoglobin** Pigment that occurs in red blood cells; binds to oxygen and carbon dioxide to carry these gases around the body.
- **platelet** Tiny disk in the blood that helps clotting.

Breathing involves the movement of gases between the body and its environment. Biologists call this gas exchange. The organs that carry out this process make up the respiratory system.

Imagine a little girl who does not get what she wants. She may threaten to "hold her breath until she's blue." After one attempt to carry out this threat, most children are smart enough not to try again. But why can't the girl hold her breath for as long as she wants? Every cell in your body needs a gas called oxygen to function. Breathing helps deliver this gas. It also takes away another gas, carbon dioxide, that is one of the waste products of a cell's functions. The little girl cannot hold her breath until she dies. Breathing is so important that it is controlled by the body's **autonomic nervous system**. This system regulates crucial body functions automatically in a way that is beyond our conscious control.

It is impossible for people to breathe underwater. Divers must use a tank containing oxygen gas and other gases to breathe.

Diffusion

Imagine a liquid in a jar separated into two halves by a membrane. One of the halves contains lots of dissolved salt; the other half has just a touch of salt. After a time the salt concentrations in each half will become equal. That is because molecules (small particles) move from places where their concentration is high to places where their concentration is low. This movement of molecules is called **diffusion**.

Oxygen is needed to break down the fuels such as glucose that power cells. As cells use up oxygen, the concentration of oxygen inside becomes lower than the concentration outside. So oxygen diffuses in through the cell membrane and into the cell. Similarly, as waste carbon dioxide builds up inside the cell, its concentration becomes higher than outside. Carbon dioxide then diffuses out through the cell membrane.

Diffusion is the key to gas exchange. Large animals with lots of cells, such as people, have respiratory systems in which oxygen and carbon

---

UNDERSTANDING DIFFUSION

Imagine two types of molecules, O and C, separated by a membrane. The concentration of Os is greater on the left, so they diffuse to the right, where there are fewer Os. The concentration of Cs is greater on the right, so they diffuse across the membrane to the left, where there are fewer Cs. In time this diffusion will lead to both sides having equal concentrations of Os and Cs.

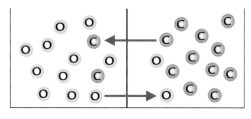

dioxide diffuse in and out of the blood. As it moves through the body, blood comes into contact with body cells. Blood transports gases between the cells and the respiratory organs, the lungs.

The passage of air

Air enters the nose or mouth and goes down a tube called the trachea. It splits into tubelike branches called the bronchi (singular, bronchus). The bronchi then enter the lungs, where they branch into even smaller tubes called the bronchioles.

Gas exchange occurs in the lung cells. Lungs contain large numbers of clusters of air sacs called alveoli (singular, **alveolus**). The alveoli bunch together like grapes at the tips of the bronchioles. Each bunch is called an alveolar sac. Because each sac contains many alveoli, the surface area available for gas exchange is enormous. The 600 million or so alveoli in a pair of human lungs have a surface area of around 750 square feet (68 sq m)—enough to cover a tennis court.

People breathe in oxygen-rich air from the environment and breathe out air laden with carbon dioxide from inside their body. The two gases are constantly being exchanged inside the alveoli. The walls of an alveolus are only one-cell thick to help swift diffusion. They are also elastic to allow easy movement of gases in and out of the air sac. Alveoli contain a network of vessels called capillaries that carry blood through the lungs. Gas exchange occurs between the blood in the capillaries and air in the alveoli. Gases move through the moist inner surface of the alveoli.

Blood movements

Blood that enters the lungs from the heart has already traveled through the body, collecting its waste products on its way. The concentration of carbon dioxide in this blood is high, while the carbon dioxide concentration in the alveoli is low. So carbon dioxide diffuses out of the blood and into the alveoli.

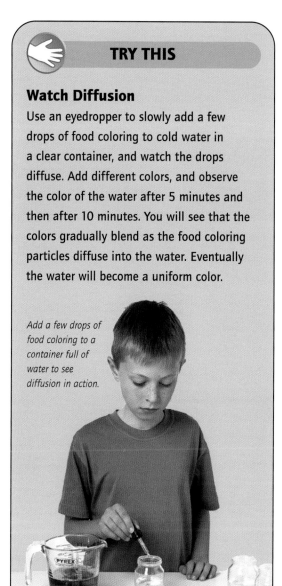

TRY THIS

Watch Diffusion
Use an eyedropper to slowly add a few drops of food coloring to cold water in a clear container, and watch the drops diffuse. Add different colors, and observe the color of the water after 5 minutes and then after 10 minutes. You will see that the colors gradually blend as the food coloring particles diffuse into the water. Eventually the water will become a uniform color.

Add a few drops of food coloring to a container full of water to see diffusion in action.

From the alveoli the carbon dioxide leaves the body along the same route that air from outside enters. It is breathed out through the nose and mouth.

The blood that gives up its carbon dioxide is oxygen poor, but it picks up oxygen as it flows through the capillaries surrounding the alveoli. Once the oxygen has diffused into the capillaries, it binds to a molecule called hemoglobin contained

THE HUMAN RESPIRATORY SYSTEM

Respiration starts as soon as you take air into your mouth. The air passes into the lungs through a tube called the trachea, which branches off into two bronchi. The bronchi divide into smaller tubes called bronchioles that spread out into the lungs. At the end of the bronchioles are sacs called alveoli, where oxygen enters the lungs and waste gases pass out.

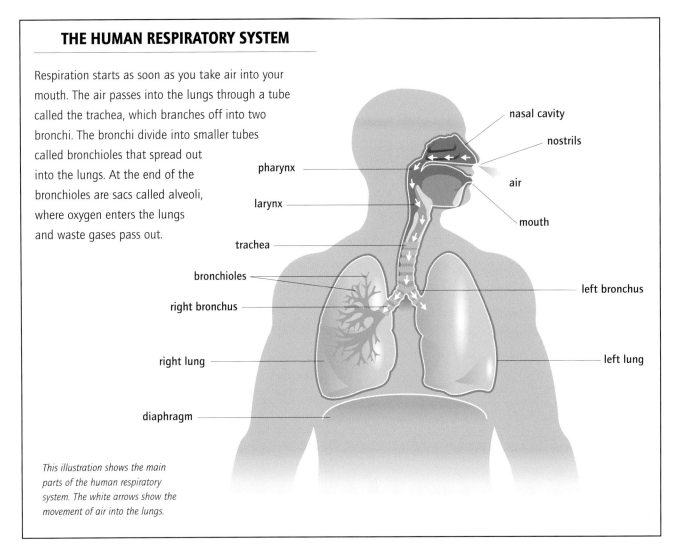

This illustration shows the main parts of the human respiratory system. The white arrows show the movement of air into the lungs.

inside red blood cells. The oxygen-rich blood then flows from the lungs back to the heart, which pumps it through the rest of the body.

When oxygen-rich blood reaches the body cells, it has a greater concentration of oxygen than they do. So the gas diffuses out of the blood by passing through the capillary membranes and into the cells. At the same time, carbon dioxide from the cells diffuses into the blood. When the blood re-enters the lungs, carbon dioxide diffuses through the alveoli and is breathed out of the body.

Cells use oxygen to respire. This involves a chemical reaction between a fuel, such as glucose, and the oxygen to produce energy.

What is hemoglobin?

Hemoglobin is the substance in red blood cells that binds to and carries oxygen to body cells. Hemoglobin has a chemical "affinity" for oxygen—that is, hemoglobin absorbs many times more oxygen than do other molecules, such as water. In fact, hemoglobin allows blood to carry 70 times more oxygen than it otherwise could. Hemoglobin is essential for efficient oxygen transport.

Looking at lungs

Human lungs are large, triangular organs that are broader at the bottom than at the top. They are enclosed in two baglike membranes called pleurae (singular, **pleura**). The inner pleura attaches to the spongy tissue of the lungs. The outer pleura is a stronger, tougher protective membrane. The lungs are protected further by the rib cage, which surrounds them.

How do people breathe?

At the base of the lungs lies the diaphragm, a strong, elastic muscle that controls breathing. The diaphragm forms a partition between the chest and the abdomen. When relaxed, the diaphragm is domed and curves upward to rest in the chest. When the diaphragm contracts, it flattens and moves lower, increasing the volume of the rib cage, which sucks air into the lungs. The contraction of the muscles between the ribs causes the rib cage to lift and move out, increasing the volume of the lungs while causing air to enter them from the bronchi.

When the diaphragm and rib cage muscles relax, the ribs move back, down, and in. The volume of the

lungs decreases, and air is forced out of the body. The person then breathes out. The diaphragm resumes its domed position inside the chest, ready for the next breath.

SCIENCE WORDS

- **alveolus** Tiny air sac that forms bunches in the lungs through which exchange of oxygen and carbon dioxide takes place.
- **autonomic nervous system** Part of the nervous system that regulates the internal functions of the body automatically.
- **diffusion** The movement of molecules of liquids and gases from points of high concentration to points of lower concentration.
- **pleura** One of a pair of delicate saclike membranes that wrap around the lungs.

CIGARETTES AND BREATHING

Smoking cigarettes and other tobacco products damages the lungs and causes fatal diseases. Antismoking regulations are becoming more common and widespread. In many places smoking is now banned in public places, such as bars, restaurants, and sports stadiums.

Second-hand cigarette smoke breathed out by smokers may harm people nearby. This is called passive smoking. Yet most smokers claim they have a right to smoke cigarettes, especially in outside places where the smoke can disperse in the air. Do you think that there is a point at which antismoking laws interfere with a citizen's right to smoke if he or she wants to? Or do you think that something that could damage other people's health should be banned outright?

Smoking cigarettes and other tobacco products damages the lungs and causes fatal diseases. Second-hand cigarette smoke breathed out by smokers may harm people nearby. This is called passive smoking.

MOVEMENT IN ANIMALS

Most animals need to move at some stage in their lives. It may be to look for food sources, to find a mate, or to escape competitors or predators.

Animal locomotion (movement) depends on the properties of muscles. They are bundles of fibers that contract to convert energy into movement. To raise your arm, for example, your bicep muscle contracts. Muscles cannot work without something to anchor to. Most human muscles anchor to bones, though some, such as the muscles in your tongue, anchor against other muscles. Insect muscles are anchored to their tough outer shells, or **exoskeletons**.

Hydrostatic skeletons

Many animals brace their muscles against a **hydrostatic skeleton**. This is a fluid-filled cavity inside the animal's body. The pressure of the fluid acts as an anchor for the muscles around it. The hydrostatic skeleton of an earthworm, for example, is divided into segments. They allow the animal to push through dirt.

This is a green basilisk. These lizards can run across the surface of a pond or river to escape predators. They do this by slapping their feet down hard and fast—they must take 20 steps each second to stay afloat!

JET PROPULSION

Some animals use hydrostatic skeletons to swim. These animals are jet powered. They squirt water in one direction, and the force propels them in the opposite direction. Jellyfish and squid are jet propeled. Dragonfly nymphs draw water into their rear ends and squirt it out to move quickly through the water. Scallops swim using a pair of jets on either side of their shell hinge.

Jet propulsion is good for short bursts of fast swimming to escape a predator or grab prey, but it is less efficient at low speeds. Squid, for example, usually get around by flapping fins that run along the sides of their bodies.

Other animals with hydrostatic skeletons loop around. Leeches have just one body cavity. They attach to the ground with suckers at each end of their bodies, then loop around the pivot.

Swimming with fins

Fish also use fins to swim. Slow swimming is powered by small red muscles that run through their trunks. For bursts of fast swimming fish use powerful banks of white muscles. Muscles contract to flex the body of a fish from side to side. In fish like eels this causes a ripple along the body. In other types of fish, such as goldfish, most of the side-to-side movement comes from the tail. Whales and dolphins also use their tails to drive themselves forward, though these mammals flap their tails up and down.

A third group of fish, mainly ones that live on reefs or in kelp beds, use their front fins as paddles to row through the water. Many other underwater animals, such as seals and turtles, are also rowers.

Creeping crawlers

Crawling animals such as slugs need mucus to move. Slugs crawl on their large, muscular foot, secreting sticky mucus from glands as they go. Waves of muscular movement run along the foot. However, the slug does not lift its foot—the mucus is too sticky to allow that. Instead, mucus acts like a solid against which the foot can push. But when the foot pushes hard enough, the mucus changes its properties to act like a liquid. That allows part of the foot to glide forward. As the pressure drops off, the mucus switches back to behaving like a solid, and the process is repeated.

Running and walking

To get around on land, many animals walk or run. Cold-blooded animals such as amphibians and reptiles have powerful bursts of activity. A crocodile leaps from the water to snatch a drinking antelope; frogs can hop explosively to avoid a predator. However, these animals are unable to sustain their bursts of activity for long. The champion runners over longer distances are the warm-blooded mammals. Although you may think mammals like cats, horses, mice, and dogs move around in different ways, their movements are actually very similar. The way an animal moves its legs is called its **gait**.

Gaits differ according to how fast an animal is moving. A horse walks slowly, speeds up to a trot, and eventually breaks into a run. A mouse does

The yellow squid can move by jet propulsion, squirting a jet of water through a hole, called the siphon, in its body. This propels the squid through the water.

HOW FAST DID DINOSAURS RUN?

Since dinosaurs died out millions of years ago, you might think figuring out how fast they could run would be an impossible task. However, English biologist Neill Alexander (born 1934) managed just that. Using modern animals, Alexander figured out how to predict an animal's speed from the distance between its footprints and the length of the leg from foot to hip.

Alexander's equations suggest that huge long-necked dinosaurs such as Brachiosaurus walked at 7.5 miles per hour (12 km/h). Large meat-eaters such as *Tyrannosaurus rex* could run at 12.5 miles per hour (20 km/h).

GLIDING THROUGH THE AIR

For animals that glide or fly, wing shape is critical. A wing forms a shape called an **airfoil**. Air pouring over the top surface of an airfoil moves more quickly than air sliding beneath its lower surface. That creates a difference in air pressure that sucks the wing upward, creating a force called **lift**. Lift opposes the weight of the animal, which pulls the animal downward. But lift alone cannot overcome another force called **drag**, caused by the resistance of the air to movement through it. Drag places a limit on how far a gliding animal can go; to remain airborne over a longer distance, an animal must be able to flap its wings.

exactly the same thing, although at much lower speeds. People switch gaits from walking to running at about 5 miles per hour (8 km/h). Birds also change gaits as they switch from slow to faster flapping flight.

Elastic tendons in the legs of the kangaroo help it save energy as it bounds. Some kangaroos can travel at speeds of up to 45 miles per hour (72 km/h) over short distances.

Saving energy

Saving energy during movement is very important. Many structures inside animals have elastic properties. They store energy as they move, then release it, so the animal uses less overall. Kangaroos have elastic tendons in their legs that snap back after they are stretched, like a rubber band. Around 40 percent of the energy used by kangaroos for hopping is saved in this way.

A much more efficient elastic material, **resilin**, occurs in the bodies of flying insects. Insects use muscles to pull down the exoskeleton (outer surface) of their midbody. That makes the wings move up. Resilin in the exoskeleton helps pull the wings down again. The insect can do this without having to use more energy moving muscles.

Getting around by gliding

Imagine a tree-living animal foraging in the forest. To save energy and avoid a trip across the ground, it makes sense to glide between the trees. Gliding has evolved many times in various animal groups. There are gliding lizards, mammals, frogs, and even fish and squid, and there were once gliding dinosaurs too. To glide, an animal needs a surface on its body that acts as a wing.

MOVEMENTS OF AIR

Why do animals like birds and butterflies flap their wings? Flapping provides a force—thrust—that acts in combination with **lift** to overcome the forces of gravity and **drag**. Each time a small bird flaps its wings, swirls of air called vortices (singular, **vortex**) leave the wing. They roll up into doughnut shapes that trail behind the animal as it flies, though people cannot see them, of course. These doughnuts, or vortex rings, also form behind flapping bats and insects. For larger birds with pointed wings, such as gulls and hawks, a different type of vortex forms. It is a tube of swirling air that follows the path of the wingtips.

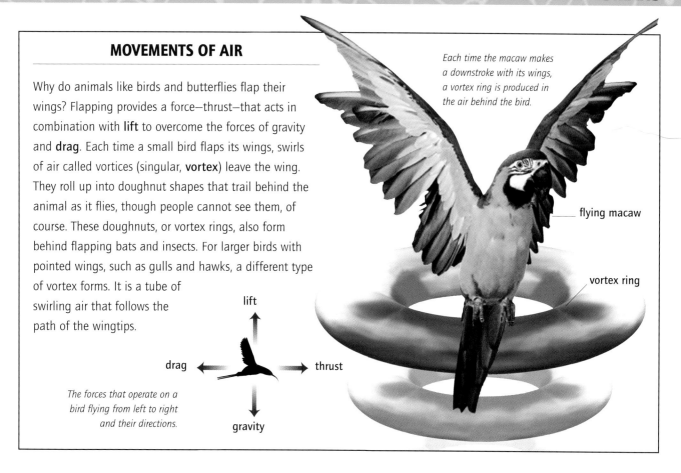

Each time the macaw makes a downstroke with its wings, a vortex ring is produced in the air behind the bird.

flying macaw

vortex ring

lift

drag

thrust

gravity

The forces that operate on a bird flying from left to right and their directions.

Powered flight

Unlike gliding, powered (or flapping) flight has evolved just a few times, in birds, insects, bats, and in extinct reptiles called pterosaurs. Flapping wings allow an animal such as a bird to overcome the effects of drag, so they can travel much farther than any glider.

Although flight uses more energy than any other form of movement, flying animals have many advantages over ground-based creatures. They can fly to catch food, escape predators, or migrate vast distances. The type of flight depends on the shape of the wings. Long wings, such as those of dragonflies and hawks, allow maneuverable flight. Shorter wings are better for faster flight, while large, long wings, such as those of albatrosses and vultures, help birds glide on rising air currents. That helps them fly many miles without wasting energy on flapping.

SCIENCE WORDS

- **airfoil** A surface that creates a force (lift) that allows animals to glide or fly.
- **drag** Force that opposes the movement of an object through water or air.
- **exoskeleton** Tough outer skin of animals such as insects.
- **gait** The way an animal moves.
- **hydrostatic skeleton** A fluid-filled structure used as a brace for muscles in many invertebrates.
- **lift** Upward force produced by airflow over a wing.
- **resilin** Chemical with elastic properties that occurs in the skins of insects.
- **vortex** A swirl of air that rolls from the wings of a flying or gliding animal.

HUMAN BONES AND MUSCLES

The bones form a framework for the body called the skeleton. Muscles are bundles of fibers that are attached to the bones. The muscles and bones work together to allow you to move.

The main functions of the skeleton are to provide support to the body, to anchor attached muscles and thus allow movement, to protect vital internal organs, and to create a constant supply of blood cells.

The skeleton

Your skeleton has two main parts. One is called the **axial skeleton**, which includes the cranium (skull), the vertebral column (backbone), and the rib cage. The other is called the appendicular skeleton, which includes the bones of the limbs, the hips, and the shoulders.

An animal's appendicular skeleton determines how it moves—for example, whether it walks on two or four legs, runs, swims, or flies.

Bones meet at joints, of which there are several kinds. Different joints allow the bones to move in different directions. Some joints, such as most in

Arm wrestlers try to outcompete each other. They are using their arm muscles and bones to prove who is the strongest.

OSTEOPOROSIS

One out of two women and one out of eight men experience bone loss as they get older. This condition is called **osteoporosis**. It can arise as a result of lack of exercise, a calcium-poor diet, or the hormonal changes that occur during and after menopause (when menstruation stops). Some doctors state that osteoporosis can be prevented if children and young adults keep up a lifelong routine of regular exercise and eat a diet rich in calcium or take calcium supplements to prevent bone loss later in life. How would you alter your diet and daily life to help prevent osteoporosis when you grow older?

your skull, permit no movement at all. You might have muscles that allow you to wiggle your ears, but there is no way you can flex your skull.

Bone

The human skeleton is made of a hard tissue called bone. Although bones vary in size and shape, they all have a similar structure. Bone consists mainly of inorganic materials, such as calcium and phosphorus, and protein fibers called collagen.

Most bone has three layers. The outer layer is called the periosteum. It is the layer from which new bone forms and the protective layer. The periosteum is riddled with blood vessels and nerve endings.

Beneath the periosteum lies the white, rock-hard compact bone that supports the body's weight. Compact bone contains a network of tiny chambers, each of which contains an osteocyte.

The innermost and least dense layer of bone is called spongy bone, or bone marrow. It is in this layer that blood cells are produced. Spongy bone contains two types of marrow. Red marrow produces blood cells, while yellow marrow stores fat.

THE HUMAN SKELETON

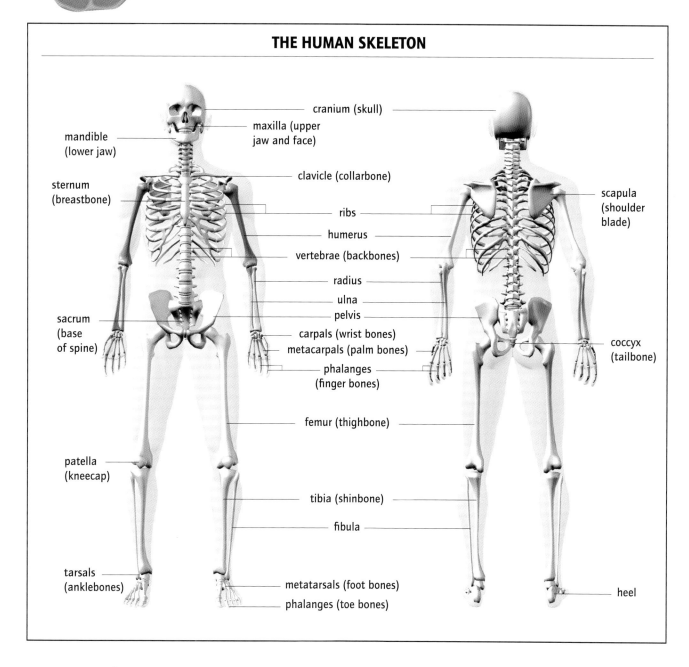

cranium (skull)

maxilla (upper jaw and face)

mandible (lower jaw)

sternum (breastbone)

clavicle (collarbone)

scapula (shoulder blade)

ribs

humerus

vertebrae (backbones)

radius

ulna

pelvis

sacrum (base of spine)

carpals (wrist bones)

metacarpals (palm bones)

coccyx (tailbone)

phalanges (finger bones)

femur (thighbone)

patella (kneecap)

tibia (shinbone)

fibula

tarsals (anklebones)

metatarsals (foot bones)

heel

phalanges (toe bones)

Bone growth

Bone is constantly being broken down and rebuilt. Three types of bone cells are involved in this process. Osteoclasts break down and dissolve old and damaged bones. Osteoblasts make new bone tissue. Osteocytes maintain the right amount of calcium and phosphorus in newly created bone.

Leg and arm bones grow, or elongate (get longer), from sites called growth plates. They are near the ends of the bones. A white, flexible tissue called cartilage occurs at the growth plates. Connective tissue forms around the cartilage, eventually turning it into compact bone. Blood vessels extend from the bone marrow into the developing bone. Bone formation continues throughout childhood. When you reach your full height and your bones are fully shaped, bone elongation stops. Although adult bones do not elongate, they can be strengthened by exercise.

Joints

Most bones meet at joints—connections that allow the bones to move a certain amount in one or more directions. There are three types of joints: immovable, partly movable, and synovial joints.

Immovable joints consist of fused bones, as in the skull. Partly movable joints like those between the vertebrae often have cartilage between them and are flexible in limited directions. Synovial joints, such as those of the shoulders, allow for a wider range of movement. Joints prevent the grinding of bone against bone when you move. Where two bones meet at a joint, there are extremely smooth layers of cartilage. Synovial joints also produce a lubricant (slippery substance) called synovial fluid. The fluid serves to lubricate all parts of the joint.

Bones that meet at a joint are held together by tough ligaments. Ligaments are a type of tough connective tissue. When people damage a ligament, they are said to have a "sprain."

Muscles

Muscles are bundles of fibers most of which are attached to and pull on your bones. In this way they move your body. They can do so because muscle cells are master shape shifters. They can change their shape by squeezing; they never push.

There are three basic types of muscles—smooth muscle, skeletal muscle, and cardiac muscle. Smooth muscles line most of your internal organs, such as your stomach and intestines. These muscles move without you willing them to because they are controlled by the autonomic nervous system.

Muscle antagonism

Most skeletal muscles work by opposing the actions of other muscles. Thus, when one muscle contracts, its opposite (the antagonist muscle) relaxes and is stretched. For example, when you lift something with your arm, nerve signals from the brain travel to your

---

THE HUMERUS

This diagram shows a cross section through a humerus, the upper arm bone.

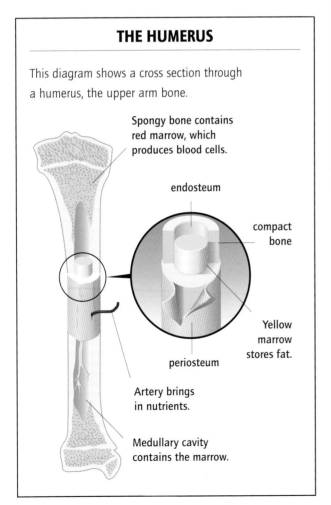

Spongy bone contains red marrow, which produces blood cells.

endosteum

compact bone

Yellow marrow stores fat.

periosteum

Artery brings in nutrients.

Medullary cavity contains the marrow.

ARTIFICIAL BONES AND JOINTS

When they are injured or diseased, entire bones or joints sometimes need to be replaced. Surgeons remove the old joint or bone (often a hip or knee) and implant a new one. In the 1920s implants were made of stainless steel. By the 1950s manufacturers of implants used pure titanium, another metal. Both materials were problematic. Body fluids damaged them, and they were not very strong or long lasting. The latest implants are made of a combination of the metals nickel and titanium called nitinol. Nitinol is not eroded by the body, and it is also very strong and flexible.

MAJOR SKELETAL MUSCLES OF THE HUMAN BODY

Skeletal muscles attach to the bones they move. They are also called voluntary muscles (because they are under your control most of the time) or striated muscles (because under a microscope they look striated, or striped).

Most muscles are attached directly to the bones in your skeleton. Many of your lip and face muscles, however, are not attached directly to bone. All muscles have lots of sensory nerves that tell the brain what a muscle is doing.

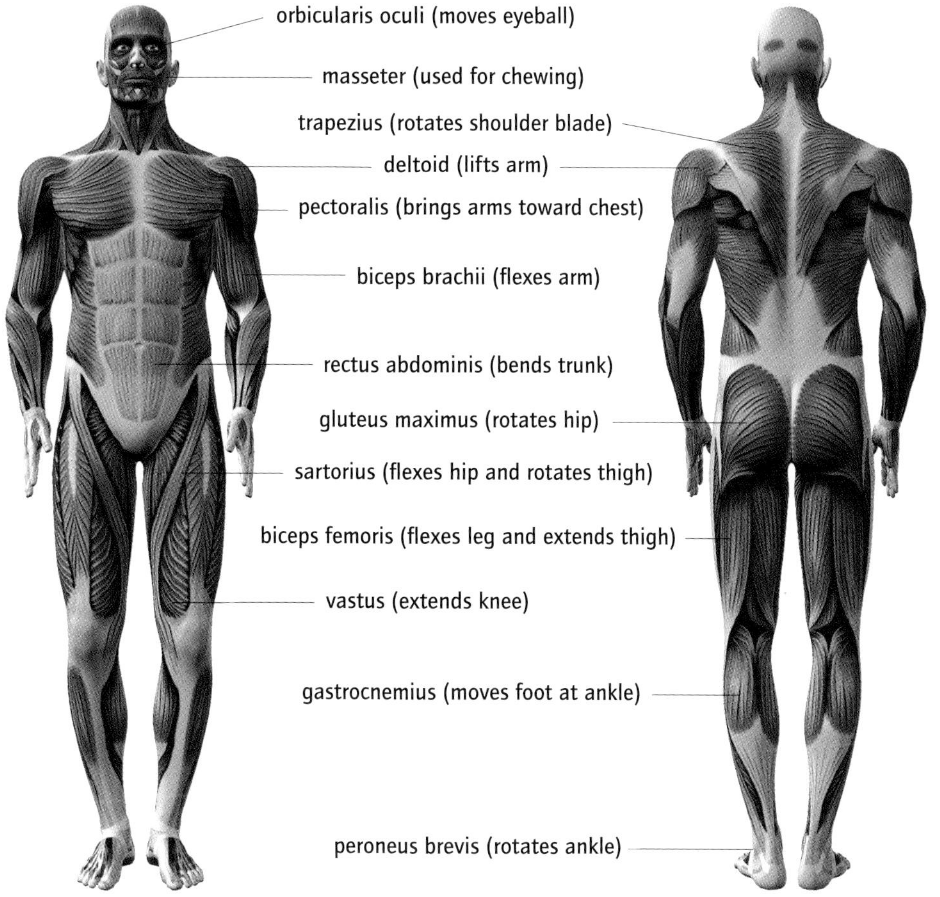

Skeletal, or voluntary, muscles control conscious movements, such as moving your arm to pick up a glass of water.

orbicularis oculi (moves eyeball)

masseter (used for chewing)

trapezius (rotates shoulder blade)

deltoid (lifts arm)

pectoralis (brings arms toward chest)

biceps brachii (flexes arm)

rectus abdominis (bends trunk)

gluteus maximus (rotates hip)

sartorius (flexes hip and rotates thigh)

biceps femoris (flexes leg and extends thigh)

vastus (extends knee)

gastrocnemius (moves foot at ankle)

peroneus brevis (rotates ankle)

arm muscles and tell the muscles on the front of your upper arm—the biceps—to contract, or flex. At the same time, the opposing muscle to the biceps on the back of your arm—the triceps—relaxes and extends to allow your arm to bend. The muscle that contracts is called the flexor muscle, and the muscle that relaxes is called the extensor muscle.

Muscle contraction

Muscles contract when they receive signals from the brain and other parts of the **central nervous system (CNS).** The signals travel along nerves called motor **neurons** from the spinal cord to muscles. Neurons release a chemical that makes the muscle contract.

SCIENCE WORDS

- **axial skeleton** Part of the skeleton consisting of the skull, backbone, and rib cage.
- **central nervous system (CNS)** The brain and spinal cord and their supporting cells.
- **neuron** A nerve cell.
- **osteoporosis** A condition leading to brittle and fragile bones that mainly affects older women.

HUMAN NERVOUS SYSTEM

Your nervous system is a huge network of 100 billion nerve cells. It coordinates how you react to events that take place around you.

The nervous system senses the outside world and helps you react to events there by thinking, moving, and speaking. It also regulates many functions inside your body, such as breathing and heart rate. Nerves contain bundles of thousands of nerve cells, or neurons. They transmit messages in the form of electrical signals that travel along their length.

Your nervous system has two main parts. They are called the central nervous system and the **peripheral nervous system**. The central nervous system, or CNS, is made up of the brain and a collection of nerve cells called the spinal cord that run along the back to the brain. The CNS also contains cells called glia that nourish and protect the neurons.

The central nervous system

The CNS acts as the body's control and processing unit. The peripheral nervous system, or PNS, is different. It consists of a network of nerves that spread from the central nervous system to other parts of the body. The PNS has two main parts, the **somatic nervous system** and the autonomic nervous system. The somatic system is concerned with the outside world and your reactions to it. It gathers information from your sense organs and sends this information to the CNS. It also carries signals from the CNS to the muscles attached to parts of your skeleton, allowing you to make conscious movements.

The autonomic system regulates the internal workings of your body. It carries information from the body to the CNS and transmits signals from the brain to organs such as the heart. Nerve cells that carry information toward the CNS are called sensory

THE NERVOUS SYSTEM

The central nervous system (CNS) is shown in red; the peripheral nervous system (PNS) is shown in blue. The somatic nervous system and the autonomic system are parts of the peripheral nervous system. A plexus is a dense network of nerves where autonomic and somatic nerves join.

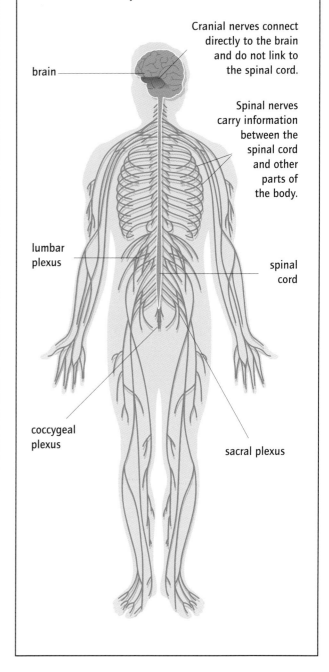

brain

Cranial nerves connect directly to the brain and do not link to the spinal cord.

Spinal nerves carry information between the spinal cord and other parts of the body.

lumbar plexus

spinal cord

coccygeal plexus

sacral plexus

TRY THIS

Test Your Response

Hold a ruler at one end, and let it hang down vertically. Have a friend put his or her hand near the bottom of the ruler with the thumb and forefinger ready to grasp it but not touching it. Tell your friend that you will drop the ruler sometime within the next 5 seconds and that he or she must try to catch it as fast as possible. Record the place at which he or she catches the ruler. This measurement will give you an idea of your friend's response time. Try this three or four times, and figure out an average response time for your friend. Then reverse roles, and test your own response time. Is the result much different between you and your friend? Try the same test at different times of day—in the morning and in the evening—to see if there is any difference in the results.

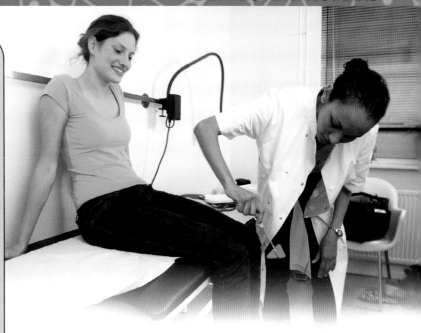

This physician is testing the reflexes of a woman. A sharp tap just below the kneecap leads to a "knee-jerk" reflex.

neurons. Those that carry signals from the CNS to organs such as muscles are called motor neurons.

Reflexes

To a large extent your nervous system works automatically by reflex action. A reflex is a predictable, automatic response of the nervous system to an event (called a stimulus) outside or inside the body. Many reflexes operate by means of nerve connections in the spinal cord and do not require any conscious involvement of the brain.

Most reflexes are defense mechanisms that protect you against injury, such as withdrawing your hand when it touches a hot surface. Some reflexes, such as blinking your eye, work by means of nerve cell connections in parts of your brain.

The brain

Your brain is a soft, rounded mass about the size of a large grapefruit. It contains two main types of tissue, called gray matter and white matter. Gray matter is mainly made up of the cell bodies of billions of interconnected nerve cells. White matter consists mainly of nerve cell fibers—cabling that connects different parts of the brain. Protective glial cells are distributed throughout the brain.

At the base of the brain is a structure called the brain stem. This stalklike organ connects the brain to the spinal cord. The brain stem is made up of three parts called the medulla, the pons, and the midbrain. The brain stem helps regulate automatic body functions such as the heartbeat and breathing. Behind the brain stem is a structure called the cerebellum. This structure helps control posture and balance, and it also coordinates movements. Thanks to your cerebellum, you can stand upright, keep your balance, and move around.

The uppermost and largest part of the brain is called the cerebrum. It is split into two halves called

THE STRUCTURE OF THE BRAIN

This vertical cross section shows the main structures inside the brain. The heavily folded cerebral cortex is where the brain processes activities such as speech.

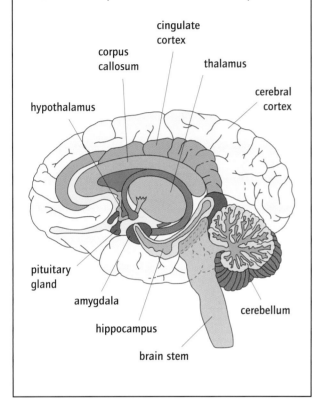

the **hypothalamus**, which forms a link between the nervous system and the endocrine system; and the limbic system, a collection of brain structures involved in functions such as memory, emotion, instinctive behavior, and sense of smell.

The brain uses up oxygen and nutrients at a fast rate in order to function, and for this reason it needs a large supply of blood. Numerous small blood vessels run throughout the brain. They are supplied by four large arteries that run up through the neck. If the blood supply to your brain were to be cut off for any reason, you would lose consciousness within ten seconds. After just a few minutes your brain would be permanently damaged.

Lobes of the cortex

Each of the brain's hemispheres contains four main regions called lobes. They are the frontal lobe (at the front), the occipital lobe (at the back), the temporal lobe (at the side), and the parietal lobe (on the upper side behind the frontal lobe). The cortex that covers each lobe has specific functions. For example,

the cerebral hemispheres. They are joined by a thick band of nerve cell fibers called the corpus callosum. The surface of each hemisphere is heavily folded, so the cerebrum looks a little like a huge walnut. The folds increase the area available for neurons. This outer part of the brain consists of gray matter and is called the cerebral cortex. The cortex is where advanced brain activities, such as thought and recognition of speech, take place.

Above the brain stem and between the two cerebral hemispheres are several other brain parts. They include the thalamus, which contains some areas involved in memory and movement; the **pituitary gland**, which produces many hormones and is an important part of the endocrine system;

BRAIN DEATH

The brain stem controls parts of the body such as the heart. With advances in medical technology physicians can sometimes keep these body parts working even when the brain stem has ceased to function. A new way of recognizing death, called brain death, was developed in the 1970s. Brain death occurs when the whole brain, including the brain stem, stops functioning, and there is no hope of getting it working again. Most doctors accept that a brain-dead person has died—there is no point in keeping that person's heart pumping. Others are uncomfortable with brain death since it goes against traditional ideas about death.

parts of the temporal lobe play a role in hearing; a large area of the frontal lobe (called the motor cortex) controls body movements; and a strip of the parietal lobe is involved in the sense of touch.

Different parts of the cortex often work together. For example, when you see someone you know, one part of the brain recognizes that person's face, and another finds the person's name in your memory. A third area analyzes your feelings about the person and whether you would like to speak to them. A fourth figures out the form of speech, and a fifth produces the sequence of nerve signals to muscles in your chest, neck, and mouth to say "hello."

Some brain functions are shared equally between the two sides of the cerebrum. For example, there is a motor cortex on each side. Each motor cortex controls movements on the opposite side of the body. Functions such as language, are handled on one side of the brain called the dominant hemisphere.

In nearly all right-handed people, and in about two-thirds of left-handed people, the left cerebral hemisphere is the dominant hemisphere. In most people the left hemisphere is also the one used for mathematical skills.

The nondominant hemisphere is important in spatial skills. People who suffer mild damage to the nondominant hemisphere may find they have problems when trying to read maps, or they may have trouble putting clothes on the right way around.

Memory and learning

One of the most important of your brain's functions is the ability to memorize information. Your brain retains a memory not just of facts, such as your name and home address, but also the meanings of those words and what those words sound and look like, the shapes and colors of objects, and so on. The brain also keeps a memory of events in your past and it memorizes skills, such as how to play the piano. The process of memorizing information and skills is called learning.

SCIENCE WORDS

- **hypothalamus** Part of the brain that releases chemicals that control the pituitary gland.
- **peripheral nervous system (PNS)** A network of nerves that spreads from the central nervous system to the rest of the body.
- **pituitary gland** Gland in the brain that releases hormones. They control the output of other endocrine glands.
- **somatic nervous system** Part of the PNS that gathers information from sensory organs and sends it to the central nervous system; also takes signals from the CNS to the muscles.

Scientists do not understand exactly how memories are stored in the brain, but they do know that there are two different types of memory storage systems. Short-term memory is for information you have just been told, such as a phone number. Information about important events and skills that you have learned by repetition go into a long-term memory bank. They generally stay with you for life.

A complex activity, such as playing the piano, requires an enormous amount of activity in the brain and in the rest of the nervous system.

HUMAN SENSES

One of your body's most important functions is to make you aware of things that are happening all around you. Detecting changes in the world is the job of the senses, which are controlled by the brain.

The human body has developed five different ways of detecting information about the world. We call them the five senses, and they are sight, hearing, smell, taste, and touch.

The first four of the senses are concentrated within single organs of the body. The fifth sense, touch, is unique since it is carried out by sensitive cells throughout the whole body, especially the skin. Detecting, or sensing, the world involves more than just the body's sense organs and sensitive cells. The nervous system carries the information that the senses detect to the brain. The brain is the body's nerve center, and it is constantly interpreting a large amount of sensory information and figuring out how to respond. A very large part of detecting what is happening in the world occurs in the brain rather than in the sense organs themselves.

Seeing

The eyes are by far the most complex and important sense organs. You have two eyes. The brain combines the two slightly different images each eye generates to make a single, three-dimensional (3-D) view of the world. This is called stereoscopic or binocular vision. Each eye is made up of an eyeball attached to six different muscles that rotate the eyeball in a socket within the skull.

The eyeball works in a similar way as a camera. Light goes through the cornea, a transparent outer lens of the eye, and the pupil, the black opening in the colored iris. The light is bent by a lens, travels through the vitreous humor (a clear gel that keeps the eyeball spherical), and arrives at the **retina**, a structure at the back of the eye.

The retina is like the photographic film in a camera. Sensory information from the retina is carried by the optic nerves (one from each eye) to the cerebral visual cortex, the part of the brain that decodes visual information. Together we call the eyes, the optic nerves, and the visual cortex the visual system.

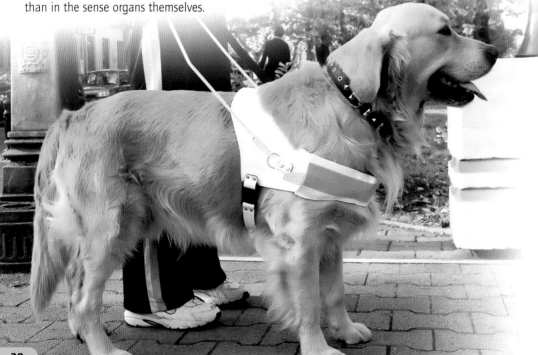

A person who has lost the sense of sight is guided by a specially trained dog. Deaf people are also helped by dogs that have been taught to alert them to sounds such as the doorbell ringing.

THE PARTS OF THE EYE

This illustration shows the main parts of the eye. Light enters the eye through the pupil and hits light-sensitive cells on the retina at the back of the eye. The cells then send messages to the brain through the optic nerve.

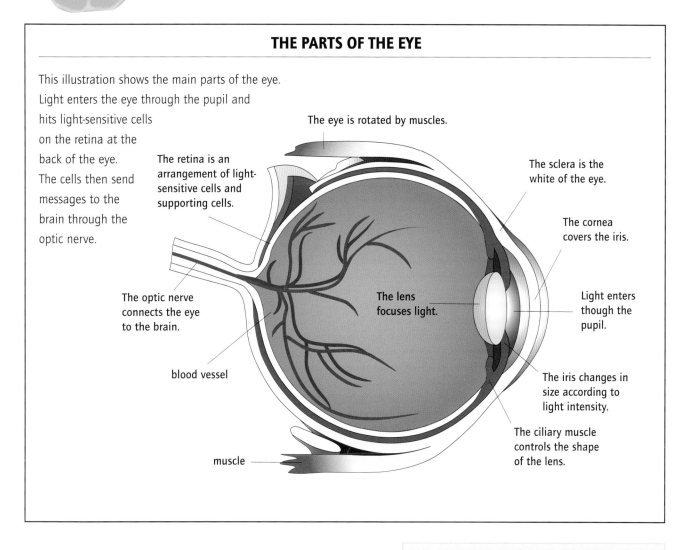

The eye is rotated by muscles.

The retina is an arrangement of light-sensitive cells and supporting cells.

The sclera is the white of the eye.

The cornea covers the iris.

The optic nerve connects the eye to the brain.

The lens focuses light.

Light enters though the pupil.

blood vessel

The iris changes in size according to light intensity.

The ciliary muscle controls the shape of the lens.

muscle

The retina is packed with two main types of cells. Some are shaped like rods and some like cones. These two cell types can detect different kinds of light. There are roughly 120 million rods and around six million cones. The rods are sensitive mainly to gray shades and dim light; the cones are sensitive to colored light. There are three types of cones, and each one is filled with a chemical that makes it most sensitive to either red, blue, or green light. The rods and cones are not distributed randomly over the retina. Most of the cones are packed into the center of the retina, called the fovea. The rods are arranged around the edge of the retina. That explains why your eyes see colors clearly in the center of what you look at (where there are most cones), and why you

HOW MANY SENSES?

Most people believe they have only five senses, but it is possible there may be as many as 15 senses or more. While the classic five senses are concerned with detecting the outside world, the other senses tell the brain what is happening inside the body. Feelings such as hunger, tiredness, and balance are examples of these internal sense mechanisms. Small organs in the inner ear control balance. They detect movements of your head and feed signals back to your brain so it can order muscles in your body to move and help you keep your balance.

see dim objects or faint movements at the edges (this is the area where there are mostly rods).

If the visual system is damaged in some way, the result can be anything from disrupted sight to complete blindness. Cataracts are a common eye problem in which part of the lens stops letting the light through due to old age, injuries, or poor diet. People who are color blind have trouble telling some colors apart because they lack one or more of the three types of cone cells.

Damage to parts of the brain that process visual information can lead to conditions called agnosias. People with an agnosia can see objects because their eyes work, but do not recognize the objects because the visual cortex in their brain is damaged.

Hearing

Hearing is essential for human communication. Without hearing it is not possible to detect speech or listen to music. Just as your two eyes produce a three-dimensional landscape of the world, so your two ears generate a kind of three-dimensional "soundscape." In this soundscape you can easily locate sounds, such as someone calling your name.

Like the visual system, the auditory (or hearing) system has sense organs (the two ears), connections between the brain and the sense organs (the auditory nerves), and a part of the brain with the job of processing sounds from the ears (the auditory cortex).

TRY THIS

Reaching Out

Sit in front of a table that has different objects on it. Close one eye. Now without moving your head, try to reach out and touch different objects. Two eyes help us judge distances and locate things. See how much harder this is when you are using only one eye.

The ear itself has three main parts: the outer ear, the middle ear, and the inner ear. The fleshy, outer part is called the pinna or auricle. It collects sounds and channels them down a curved pipe, called the auditory canal, toward a structure called the tympanic membrane (eardrum).

When sound waves enter the ear, they make the air move back and forth in the auditory canal, and that causes the eardrum to vibrate. Three small bones called the malleus (hammer), incus (anvil), and stapes (stirrup), which look a bit like the objects they are named for, are connected to the eardrum, and they vibrate as well. Their vibrations are carried through a tiny membrane called the oval window to the passage and structures of the inner ear. The most important part of the inner ear is a

NIGHT SIGHT

Police officers and soldiers use night-vision cameras to help them see in the dark. Just as your eyes are sensitive to the light things give off, these cameras detect an invisible kind of light called infrared radiation. Animals or people are warmer than their surroundings and show up as red or purple on infrared cameras. The hand in the picture opposite is warmer than the object he is holding, so it shows up as red and purple.

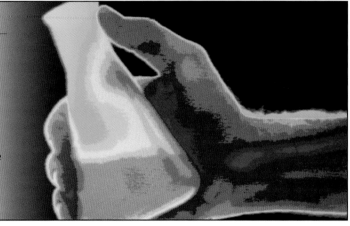

THE HEARING SYSTEM

Sound waves pass through the auditory canal and vibrate the tympanic membrane (eardrum). The ossicles transmit vibrations of the tympanic membrane to the oval window on the outside of the cochlea. The cochlea contains a liquid. When it receives vibrations, nerve endings in the cochlea are stimulated and send signals to the brain to be interpreted.

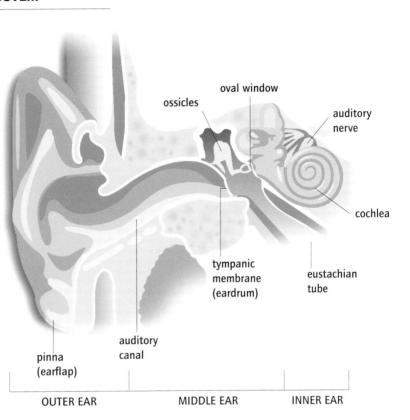

oval window

ossicles

auditory nerve

cochlea

tympanic membrane (eardrum)

eustachian tube

auditory canal

pinna (earflap)

OUTER EAR   MIDDLE EAR   INNER EAR

structure shaped like a snail shell called the **cochlea**, which is filled with fluid and has 15,000 sensitive hairs on its walls. As sound vibrations travel from the oval window to the cochlea, they make the fluid move. The hairs detect the movement of the fluid and generate nerve impulses in the auditory nerve. The nerve carries the signals to the brain, which interprets them as recognizable sounds.

The other senses

Touch, taste, and smell are other vital senses. Touch or sensation comes from sensitive nerve endings in the skin and from the hairs nearby. They respond to factors of pressure, pain, and temperature. Taste comes from taste buds, which are extremely sensitive bumps on the tongue. Smell is detected by seven types of receptor cells inside the nose that are

sensitive to roughly seven different types of smells. The receptor cells send signals down the olfactory (smell) nerves to parts of the brain that specialize in recognizing smells.

SCIENCE WORDS

- **cochlea** Coiled, fluid-filled structure in the inner ear that translates vibrations received at the tympanum into signals that go to the brain.
- **retina** Sensitive layer of cells at the back of the eye that is stimulated by light. It sends this visual information to the brain through the optic nerve.

COPING WITH THE ENVIRONMENT

Animals live almost everywhere on Earth—in rivers, lakes, and oceans, in the air, on land, and in the soil.

The type of place where an animal lives is called its habitat. Animals like rats, foxes, and cockroaches are generalists—adaptable creatures able to thrive in many habitats. Most animals, however, are adapted to live in just one particular habitat and cannot survive elsewhere. For example, most penguins are suited to life in and around cold southern seas, and could not survive in a desert. Some animals begin life in one environment and move to another as adults. Adult toads can live on land, but they develop from water-dwelling tadpoles.

Life in cold places

The polar regions are one of the harshest habitats on Earth, with bitterly cold temperatures except during the brief summer and up to six months'

darkness each year. Land in these areas is permanently covered with a thick sheet of ice. For much of the year the seas are also covered with ice, but they abound with animals such as whales, seals, and fish. Such diversity relies on **plankton**, which thrive in the nutrient-rich waters. Polar bears and penguins live and breed on floating sea ice or on coasts. However, just a few tiny animals, such as springtails and roundworms, can survive inland.

South of the Arctic lie the barren, treeless lowlands of the tundra. Here winters are also long and very cold, but summers are warmer, with long hours of light. Arctic foxes and hares, lemmings, and snowy owls are among the few species that live on the tundra all year round. Other animals, such as caribou, migrate there in spring to breed.

Animals of polar and near-polar lands have physical features that help them withstand the harsh

Emperor penguins raise their chicks on the ice of Antarctica, one of the most inhospitable places on Earth.

AMAZING MIGRATIONS

Many animals avoid harsh conditions by making long, seasonal journeys called **migrations**. They may travel thousands of miles to avoid winter weather, find food, or reach a safe place to breed. Caribou, whales, monarch butterflies, salmon, eels, and turtles are all famous migrants. Many North American birds, such as hummingbirds, waders, and geese, migrate south for the winter. The champion migrants, however, are Arctic terns, which fly up to 20,000 miles (32,000 km) as they shuttle between the Arctic and Antarctic each year.

The monarch butterfly makes an amazing two-way journey each year.

→ migration route
▢ summer range
▢ winter range

climate. Mammals such as musk oxen, Arctic foxes, and polar bears have thick, hairy coats to keep them warm. Arctic foxes also have hairy feet and small ears that help conserve body heat. Aquatic creatures such as seals and penguins have thick layers of blubber just under the skin that provide insulation.

Life in deserts

Lack of moisture is the main problem in deserts. They are places that receive less than 10 inches (25 cm) of rain each year. These harsh habitats also have extreme variations in temperature. Most deserts are boiling hot by day and freezing cold at night; high-altitude deserts are cold most of the time. Food and shelter are also scarce. Despite this, a surprising number of animals live in deserts, including a range of insects, spiders, scorpions, and reptiles, and also many mammals and birds.

Desert mammals have pale fur that reflects the Sun and provides good **camouflage**. Desert hares and foxes have large ears that radiate body heat, helping the animal keep cool, while Cape ground squirrels use their long bushy tails as portable sunshades. Sand cats, addax antelope, and web-footed geckoes

have broad feet to keep them from sinking into the sand. Camels have many adaptations to desert life, including broad feet and long eyelashes to keep out sand. Their single or double hump acts as a fat store. These animals can survive for days without water.

Finding water

Desert creatures such as burrowing owls, lizards, and snakes spend the hot midday hours in cool burrows or in the shade of rocks. They emerge to search for food at dusk, when temperatures drop. Most desert animals get all the moisture they need from their food, so they do not need to drink. However, there is usually some water available in even the driest desert—in the cool of the early morning dew often forms. Some animals can exploit this precious resource. Desert beetles allow dew to collect on their bodies. One of the most effective dew collectors is an Australian lizard called a moloch. This animal is covered with sharp spines to fend off predators. Running along the spines are a series of grooves that channel moisture along the animal's body and into the corner of its mouth.

Forest life

Forests and woodlands offer animals shelter from the elements and good sites to nest and hide from enemies. The abundance of plant life attracts a wide range of plant eaters, which attract predators in turn. The cold pine forests of the north are home to fewer species than temperate woodlands, where trees lose their leaves in fall. In both these habitats food is scarce in winter, so some animals hibernate, while others migrate. Tropical rain forests grow nearer the equator. There the climate is always warm and wet, and plant life remains lush all year round. Rain forests contain a greater variety of life than any other habitat.

In rain forests the canopy—the layer of leaves highest above the ground—is home to the greatest number of species. Canopy animals are either fliers such as bats, birds, and insects or skilled climbers such as squirrels and monkeys. Many monkeys and other canopy mammals have a gripping tail that acts

This fennec fox is superbly adapted for desert life. Its pale colors reflect heat and provide camouflage, while its burrow gives shelter from the Sun. The fox can lose heat quickly through its enormous ears.

WHAT IS A BIOME?

Biomes are vast groupings of habitats. For example, regions in the world with very low rainfalls are grouped into the desert biome. Habitats are more specific. The Sonoran desert, with its giant cacti and its other distinctive plants, forms a habitat. Habitats can be broken down too, into microhabitats. Animals living around the roots of giant saguaro cactus live in a microhabitat.

as a climbing aid. A few animals, such as flying squirrels, can glide between trees by spreading flaps of skin to act as a wing. Other animals, including deer, pigs, and rodents such as agoutis, are adapted to life on the shady forest floor. They often feed on food dropped by canopy animals or on fruit and seeds that fall from the trees above.

Grassland animals

Grasslands occur naturally in regions that are too dry for forests, yet are moist enough for grasses to grow. The world's biggest grasslands are in east Africa, where large herds of grazing mammals such as zebras and gazelles feed on grasses, while giraffes and elephants browse on isolated trees.

Grasslands offer little cover for animals, so ground squirrels, reptiles, and some birds burrow underground. Tropical grasslands have rainy and dry seasons. Grassland mammals may migrate long distances in search of food and water in the dry season.

Ocean life

Oceans provide a variety of habitats for wildlife. Warm, sunlit coastal waters and coral reefs offer favorable conditions, and life can be very abundant in these places. However, underwater life also thrives in less favorable environments, including the open ocean, where there is no place to hide from enemies.

HIBERNATION AND DIAPAUSE

In temperate and cool climates many animals ride out harsh winter weather by entering the deep sleep of **hibernation**. Body processes such as heart rate and breathing slow down, and the animal's body temperature drops dramatically. This strategy saves energy that would otherwise be lost searching for scarce food in the cold. When the weather warms up, the animal becomes active again. Bats, ground squirrels, dormice, snakes, tortoises, and amphibians such as toads hibernate. Many insects enter a similar state of suspension called diapause to help them survive winter, famine, or drought.

Barbastelle bats hibernate in huge colonies over the winter and emerge to feed when the weather gets warmer.

Predators such as tuna, sharks, and dolphins hunt shoals of herring and mackerel that feed on plankton there. The gloomy ocean depths are a more hostile habitat. Fish, starfish, sponges, and other animals there must cope with total darkness and the great pressure caused by the waters above. The deep sea is also very cold. In polar seas some fish have a natural antifreeze in their blood that prevents their tissues from freezing.

Food in the deep ocean is often scarce. Most animals feed on dead and decaying material drifting down from the waters above. Predators such as gulper eels have huge mouths and stretchy stomachs so they can swallow any prey they come across.

Life in freshwater

Freshwater rivers, lakes, and swamps make rich habitats for fish, shellfish, amphibians, turtles, waterfowl, and many other animals. Creatures that inhabit fast-flowing streams must be strong swimmers to avoid being swept away. In some aquatic habitats such as swamps the water may become very low in oxygen or even dry up

completely. A few fish, such as mudskippers and climbing perch, can survive out of water for a time. A lungfish copes by burrowing into the mud at the bottom of a pool when it begins to dry up. Safely encased in a cocoon of mucus, the lungfish estivates. The fish can survive like this for years, until the pond begins to fill with water again.

SCIENCE WORDS

- **camouflage** A pattern of coloration that allows an animal to blend in with its surroundings.
- **hibernation** To spend the winter in an inactive or dormant state.
- **migration** Long-distance journey by animals such as birds to warmer places during winter weather.
- **plankton** Tiny animals, often the young of larger creatures, that float in the surface waters of the ocean.

DEFENSE

Animals defend themselves in a variety of ways. Defense is crucial to ensure survival until as many young as possible have been produced.

Animals need to protect themselves from predators if they are to survive and breed. Some animals rely on speed to get away; others hide and blend into the background. Some have chemical defenses, while many animals that lack these chemicals pretend to have them. There are animals that protect themselves with physical defenses, such as horns

The chameleon is a master of disguise. It can change the color of its skin to closely match its surroundings.

and tusks. Some animals build protective structures, while others rely on behavioral adaptations to keep predators at bay.

Escape is often the best means of defense. A fleeing gazelle, for example, can run from all but the most agile predator. Many animals opt to escape into the air. Tiny animals called springtails launch themselves upward with a catapult-like appendage on their bodies. Most birds and insects can fly to safety, while flying lizards drop from the trees to glide from danger. Flying fish escape underwater predators by leaping above the water and gliding, often for hundreds of feet.

Color

Other creatures prefer to hide from trouble. Their colors blend into the background, making them hard to see. This is called camouflage. Chameleons and cuttlefish can even change color to match their surroundings. Decorator crabs go one step further and actually become part of the scenery. They plant sea squirts and sea anemones on their shells to help them blend in. Many birds also rely on camouflage. Bitterns live in reed beds. Their colors match the reeds closely. When the birds are startled, they stretch their necks upward to look even more like the plants that surround them.

SMOKE SCREENS

When in danger, a squid releases an inky black liquid from a sac in its body. The liquid clouds the water, forming a smoke screen that allows the animal to escape. Squid ink is prized as a food coloring and flavoring in Mediterranean cooking. Sea hares, a group of sea slugs, release a bright purple ink into the water when threatened. Their smoke screen is more of a warning, since sea hares are rich with poisons. Their ink warns enemies not to eat them.

STINKY SKUNKS

Skunks are famous for the foul-smelling chemical spray they can produce when threatened. The skunk releases the chemicals, which can cause sickness and sting the eyes, from glands near its anus. The stinky spray can travel up to 9 feet (3 m)!

Mimicry

Some small animals hide by pretending to be objects. Many jumping spiders pretend to be bird droppings, jewel beetles look like drops of dew on a leaf, and leafhoppers look like thorns on a stem. Copying something else like this is called **mimicry**.

The champion mimics are stick and leaf insects. These animals are amazing mimics of leaves and other plant material. In addition to a leaf-shaped body some leaf insects have legs shaped like leaflets, and they sway their bodies just like a leaf in the breeze.

Chemical protection

Many small animals are protected by chemicals inside their bodies. They make the animal taste bad or make it poisonous. Some animals, such as stink bugs, are able to produce powerful smells.

Rather than hide away, chemically protected animals often advertise their bad taste with bright warning colors. Warning colors generally include yellows, reds, and black. Many animals, such as some poison arrow frogs, warn predators with bright blues and greens. A predator that eats a bad-tasting animal learns to avoid these warning colors in the future. Insects often get defensive chemicals from plants they eat when they are young. Monarch

butterflies, for example, eat poisonous milkweed plants when they are caterpillars.

Some larger animals use defensive poisons too. When ribbed newts are threatened, they pierce their own skin with their poison-tipped ribs. The duck-billed platypus has small poison spurs on its hind legs. There is even a species of poisonous bird. The hooded pitohui from New Guinea has poison-coated feathers.

Mimicking other animals

Some animals defend themselves by looking just like poisonous species. Biologists call this **Batesian mimicry**. Flatworms, sea slugs, and even fish mimic poisonous sea cucumbers, for example. Dangerous stinging animals, such as ants, wasps, and bees, also have many mimics. Harmless hoverflies, for example, look just like wasps.

Sometimes, several different poisonous species share an almost identical coloration and pattern. This is called Müllerian mimicry. Many species of tropical butterflies are Müllerian mimics. If a predator takes a bite out of a poisonous butterfly, it will avoid all similar butterflies in the future. By sharing an easy-to-recognize coloration, all the Müllerian mimics profit from the protection gained by the predator's unpleasant experience.

Sticky defenses

Some small animals use glues to stop attackers in their tracks. Threatened ladybugs squeeze blood from their leg joints. The sticky blood gums up enemies. Soldiers of one species of termite contain giant glue glands. During battle with an ant a soldier makes itself explode. Its violent death releases the glue, trapping the ant and allowing other termites to kill it. Velvet worms also use glue, but they spit it from their mouthparts.

Spitting for safety

Defensive spitting is not limited to glue. Some animals spit poisonous venom to ward off attackers. A spitting cobra rears up and drips venom from its fangs. It then breathes out hard to spray the venom at the enemy. Another spitter is the black fat-tailed scorpion. It squirts a jet of venom from the bulb at the tip of its long tail.

Spiders, snakes, and other venomous animals do not generally use their venom to drive off attackers. Venom is used only as a last resort; a "dry" bite usually does the trick. However, some venomous animals are swift to give a deadly bite.

Physical defenses

Most animals defend themselves with physical defenses, including hairs, spines, shells, and protective armor. When South American tarantulas are threatened, they shake their bodies quickly. That releases a cloud of fine hairs that irritates the nose and mouth of an attacker. Hairs have evolved into spines in many animals. Porcupines have an array of needle-sharp quills. Hedgehogs are also spiny. They have the added benefit of being able to roll themselves up into a ball. Many animals with tough or spiky outer coverings roll up into a ball. That can present a wall of inpenetrable armor to a predator. Pill bugs roll up at the first sign of danger, as do armadillos. Tortoises draw their head and limbs into their tough shells.

Super shells

Tortoise shells are based on modified rib bones. Many other animals have shells that are formed from chemicals drawn from water or food. Mussels and clams use powerful muscles to hold their shells closed tightly. Snails can draw their whole bodies into their shells, sealing the hole with a lid called

---

SOUND DEFENSE

For some animals sound is just as important as color in defense. Madagascar hissing cockroaches squeeze out air to make a fierce hissing sound. One type of grasshopper, when grasped by a predator, lets out a powerful, high-pitched chirp. The sound shocks the predator into dropping the insect. Rattlesnakes are venomous and do not wait to be attacked before sending out a warning sound. They shake horny scales on their tails to warn an enemy to keep well away.

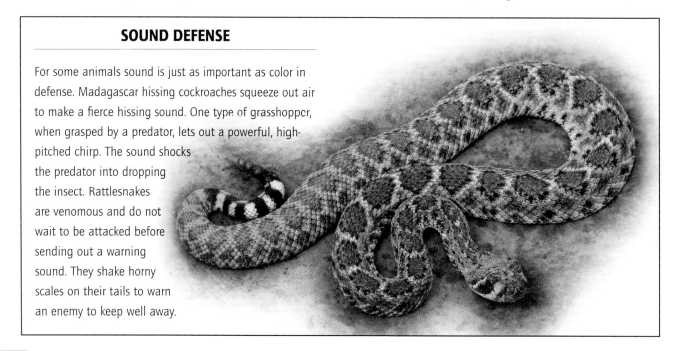

The porcupine has a formidable defensive coat of prickly quills that defend it from predators such as lions.

an operculum. Nautilus shells are extra tough, both to deter predators and to withstand the enormous pressure in the ocean depths where they live.

Other animals have more active physical defenses. Deer and antelope have horns that can be used to deter predators. Horses and giraffes use their powerful hind legs to kick out against any attacking animal, while hippos use their massive teeth to drive away other animals.

Building barriers

Sometimes physical defenses are not enough, and animals put barriers in place to keep predators at bay. Many insects form galls—bumps of plant tissue—under which they can drink plant sap in safety. Scale insects feed on the surface of plants, but coat themselves with a layer of tough wax. Spider mites spin silken webs to keep enemies out, while caddisfly **larvae** live inside protective cases they make from sand or gravel.

Behavioral defenses

Other defensive strategies involve the ways animals behave. For many mimics it is not enough to just look like another animal; they must act like them as well. Drone flies mimic honeybees. The flies fly at the same speed as the bees and take off from flowers at the same angle. Desert stink beetles stand on their heads and squirt foul-smelling liquid at enemies.

Size can also intimidate enemies. Cats arch their bodies and make their hair stand up when faced with a dog; toads and pufferfish can inflate their bodies, making them look bigger and fiercer.

A common behavioral defensive adaptation is herding. Herds often consist of several different species. On an east African savanna, for example, a herd may contain wildebeest, gazelles, zebras, and ostriches. Animals form herds because many eyes are more likely to spot a predator than a solitary animal.

Herds are also better able to fight off attacks. Musk oxen form herds on the North American tundra. When attacked by a wolf pack, adult musk oxen form a circle around the young and drive off the wolves with their horns. Similarly, birds such as terns team up to drive away a crow or gull that comes too close to their nesting site. Owls, buzzards, and other birds of prey are often chased by groups of smaller birds, too—that is called **mobbing**.

SCIENCE WORDS

- **Batesian mimicry** When a nonpoisonous animal looks similar to a different, poisonous species.
- **larva** The young of certain types of insects.
- **mimicry** Imitation of an object or another animal.
- **mobbing** When small birds team up to drive away predators or egg thieves.

BREEDING

Animals exist to breed and produce young. They do so by attracting mates, driving off rivals, courting, and mating. Some animals look after their eggs and young too.

The most important part of any animal's life is reproduction. There are two ways to do this: **asexual reproduction** and sexual reproduction. Some animals that reproduce asexually, such as hydras, produce buds that grow from their bodies. The buds eventually break away to form a new animal. Other animals, such as flatworms, can produce young by breaking off fragments. Each worm fragment grows into a complete new animal.

Other animals reproduce sexually. This involves male sex cells, or sperm, fertilizing (fusing with) female sex cells called eggs to produce young. Some animals, like slugs, contain both male and female sex organs and can reproduce with themselves.

Animals like these are called **hermaphrodites**. Other animals, such as people, have separate sexes. Breeding is the process by which such animals find and mate with others, lay eggs or give birth, and sometimes care for their young.

Where to fertilize?

The eggs of many underwater animals are fertilized outside the body in the water. These creatures release sperm and eggs into the water, where they mix and fuse. The resulting young often drift for a time as plankton before settling on the sea bottom. The release of eggs and sperm is closely timed to minimize waste. The breeding cycles of many underwater worms, for example, are regulated by the phases of the moon.

Other animals minimize waste further by fertilizing eggs inside the female's body. To do this, animals must attract a mate. Most animals then go through **courtship**. This allows the animals to indicate that each would make a good parent.

Courtship and mating

Most animals display to each other before mating takes place. These displays involve detailed movements as well as the release of chemicals. Some animals give their mates gifts. Some scorpion

A swan tends to its clutch of eggs. Swans lay only one clutch each year, and there are between three and eight eggs in a typical clutch.

flies, for example, steal dead insects from spiderwebs and present them to females before mating. This is risky and many males are caught by the spiders.

Mating involves sperm moving from the male into the body of the female. This is done in a variety of ways. Male scorpions dance the female over a package of sperm laid on the ground, called a **spermatophore**, that enters her body along a duct. Spiders deposit sperm on a sheet of silk, then use a mouthpart to suck some up. This mouthpart is inserted into the female. Male bedbugs have an altogether different method—they simply snip a hole in a female's body wall and dump sperm inside.

Birds and reptiles have a pair of organs called intromittent organs that guide the sperm into the female. Mammals have a similar organ called the penis. A male bee pops a mating structure called an

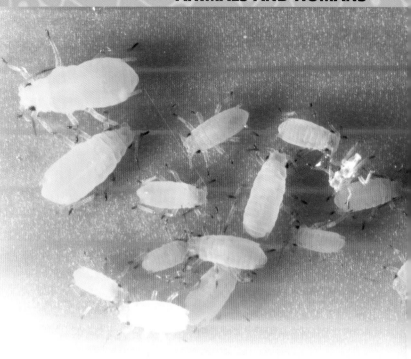

Aphids are unusual animals because they can reproduce both sexually and asexually.

ASEXUAL OR SEXUAL?

Asexual reproduction allows populations to grow quickly. Also, an asexual reproducer passes 100 percent of her **genes** on, rather than half as in sexual reproduction. Yet the vast majority of animals reproduce sexually. Why is this? The DNA (genetic code) of young produced sexually forms new combinations that differ from those of the parents. That leads to more genetic variety. This is important if a species has to evolve to cope with a new challenge, such as the appearance of a new parasite. Individuals that can survive the challenge produce young that can also survive. An asexual species might be wiped out before a response to the threat can evolve. Some animals manage to get the best of both worlds. Aphids reproduce asexually in spring to increase numbers. Later generations in the fall reproduce sexually. They lay eggs that survive winter before hatching in spring.

endophallus out from his body. It enters the female through a duct in her body; once inside, sperm explodes out. Then the endophallus snaps away and blocks the duct. This stops other males from mating with the female later.

Laying eggs

Most animals lay eggs, with the young developing inside the eggs for a time before hatching. Many insects lay their eggs in a safe place close to a good food source before leaving them to survive alone. Mantis eggs develop inside a tough case called an **ootheca**, while lacewings lay their eggs at the end of long stalks to keep them away from foraging ants.

Many animals carry their eggs with them. Nursery-web spiders lay eggs in a tough case that they carry with their mouthparts. Male midwife toads wind strings of eggs between their feet, where they protect them and keep them moist. Some cichlid fish take their eggs, which are fertilized in the water, back into their bodies. They collect the eggs in their mouths, where they hatch and the young develop.

PERILOUS MATING

Some female mantises eat their partners during mating. They eat the heads first, but the male is able to continue to mate. This may seem disastrous for the male, but his sacrifice is not in vain. His body provides a good food source for the female, allowing her to produce more eggs containing his genetic material. Such cannibalism usually occurs late in the season, when the males stand little chance of mating again. Earlier in the year they are more cautious.

A need for heat

The eggs of many animals must be kept warm during development. Some, such as crocodiles, build a mound of decaying vegetation and lay their eggs inside. Rotting creates heat that keeps the eggs warm. Turtles bury eggs in warm sand, while the Maleo megapode bird lays eggs in holes in the soil. This bird relies on geothermal heat rising from

The female praying mantis often eats the male as they start to mate. This provides the female with nutrients, which help raise her young.

deep underground. However, most birds incubate (keep warm) their eggs by sitting on them in a nest and warming them with their body heat. A female python incubates her eggs by coiling around them and vibrating her body. The heat generated by her muscles keeps the eggs warm.

Giving birth

Many animals do not lay eggs at all. Instead, the eggs stay inside their bodies but hatch just before the young are born. However, the young get all the nourishment they need from food supplies inside the egg, not from the mother. Animals such as boas, manta rays, and pill bugs produce young in this way.

Most mammals also give birth to live young, although in this case there is no shelled egg from which they hatch. In marsupials such as koalas the young leave the body very early in their development. They climb into a pouch on the mother's body and attach to a teat to suckle milk.

In placental mammals, the group that includes humans, young leave the body at a much more advanced stage. Female placental mammals need to nourish their young inside their bodies. An organ, the **placenta**, grows to do so. Food and oxygen move through the placenta from the mother's blood, while waste products from the young go the other way. Some other animals, including velvet worms, sharks, and tsetse flies have an organ similar to a placenta for nourishing young.

Raising young

After giving birth, mammals feed their young with milk. Milk is produced by the mammary glands. It is full of nutrients that the young need to grow quickly. Milk varies in composition depending on the species. Seal milk, for example, contains 60 percent fat. That helps the seal pup lay down a thick layer of blubber under its skin.

Mammals are the only animals that produce milk, although a few other animals feed their

Primates, such as these squirrel monkeys, invest a lot of energy caring for their young to ensure their survival.

young with liquids from their bodies. Pigeons produce a nutritious liquid from their crops (part of the foregut). Flamingo chicks are also fed a milky liquid from the parents' foregut.

Other animals that care for their young bring food to them from elsewhere. Carrion beetles protect their grubs until they molt. They feed them chewed up morsels of dead animal food. Birds such as gulls carry food to their nests inside their crops. The birds regurgitate (vomit) food for the chicks to eat.

PROBLEMS WITH IMPRINTING

Imprinting can cause problems, especially in captive-breeding programs to increase numbers of rare animals. Captive-bred California condors, for example, are fed by conservation workers wearing gloves shaped and colored just like an adult condor. Young condors are not exposed to humans at all. This keeps the rare youngsters from imprinting on people. Otherwise, the birds would not regard people as a threat after their release into the wild.

Incubating eggs and raising young usually need two parents. One guards the nest; the other looks for food. Parent animals may reinforce their bond through displays. For example, albatrosses perform incredible displays of honking, toe pointing, head shaking and bobbing, and bill clacking.

SCIENCE WORDS

- **asexual reproduction** Production of young without the need for mating or the fusion of sex cells.
- **courtship** Display between a male and a female prior to mating.
- **gene** Section of DNA that codes for the structure of a protein.
- **hermaphrodite** Animal with both male and female sexual organs.
- **ootheca** Egg-case of insects such as mantises.
- **placenta** Organ that develops during pregnancy and supplies the growing young with food and oxygen, and takes away waste.
- **spermatophore** A package containing sperm.

Animals constantly interact with other species. Many also live in groups with others of their own kind.

A bull moose wanders the North American forests alone. Occasionally he fights a rival male or mates with a female, but the rest of the time he keeps himself to himself. Moose are solitary (they live alone) and might not spend time with other moose, but they do carry around communities of fleas and lice. Any such relationship between species, such as the moose and its fleas, is called a **symbiosis**.

Types of symbioses

There are three types of symbioses. They are called mutualisms, commensalisms, and parasitisms. The relationship is called a **mutualism** if both species

An oxpecker picks fleas and ticks from a warthog's hide. This is a mutualism—the warthog benefits from the removal of pesky parasites, while the oxpecker gets an easy meal.

benefit. The Egyptian plover is a small bird that willingly hops inside the jaws of Nile crocodiles. The bird does not get eaten. That is because Egyptian plovers are crocodile dentists. They eat leeches and bits of meat that collect around the crocodile's teeth. The plover gets a meal, and the crocodile has its teeth cleaned.

Many animals share a close relationship with bacteria. During the day the bobtailed squid hides in sand on the seafloor. It comes out to feed at night. Swimming around on moonlit nights, it would cast a black silhouette against the sky, which a predator might spot. But the squid has a trick up its sleeve. The squid has organs on its body that provide a home for bacteria. In return the bacteria produce light that shines downward from the squid. Without a silhouette the squid is cleverly camouflaged against the sky.

Pesky parasites

Some relationships see one animal suffering at the expense of another. They are called parasitisms. Virtually every animal species on earth suffers from parasites. Parasites live on the outer surface or inside the body of other organisms called **hosts**. Fleas, lice, ticks, tapeworms, flukes, and viruses are all types of parasites.

Most parasites get free food at the expense of their hosts. Fleas and ticks bite through the host's skin to suck blood. Aphids draw sap from the veins of plant leaves. Tapeworms live in the guts of their hosts and steal partly digested food, while tiny follicle mites sip oils that keep the host's skin supple.

Finding new hosts

One of the biggest problems parasites face is how to get from host to host. Tapeworm eggs need to be swallowed by a suitable host before they can develop in the host's gut. The chances of this happening for any one egg are very remote; tapeworms counter this by producing millions of eggs in their lifetimes.

USING ANOTHER SPECIES

Often one species benefits from an association, but the other is unaffected. This is called a **commensalism**. The remora fish has a very strong sucker, which it uses to attach itself to whales, sharks, and turtles. The remora gets a free ride and may feed on scraps of uneaten food, but the swimming animal providing the taxi service is not harmed.

Even an adult sheep botfly, which can get around by flying, has to deposit its young in a suitable spot. Female sheep botflies hover in front of a sheep's head. They then shoot their bodies forward and squirt larvae (young) up the sheep's nose. The young live inside spaces in the sheep's head. After months of development the larvae drop back out through the nostrils to the soil. There they change into adults.

Wasps of death

If you were a farmer, you wouldn't be too pleased to find bugs eating your crops. What would you do? One solution is to reduce pest numbers with killer parasites, called parasitoids. That is biological control. Many parasitic wasps are parasitoids.

These insects are good biological control agents since most target just one species of insect. The wasps lay eggs inside pests such as caterpillars and aphids. The eggs hatch, and the young wasps begin to munch their hosts' internal organs. When the host dies, the wasps become adult before emerging. Then they fly away to mate and find new hosts. The wasps help keep pest numbers under control.

Group living

From shoals of silvery sardines to flocks of pink flamingos, many animals live with others of their species in groups. Like people, animals often live with relatives, while large groups may contain unrelated animals as well.

Group living can lead to competition for food and the spread of disease, but it does offer safety from predators. On African savannas herds of gazelles graze peacefully, but every few seconds a gazelle checks for signs of danger. With many pairs of eyes a large herd is more likely to spot predators like lions or a cheetah. Other animals cooperate to rear young or hunt for food. Ostriches pool their chicks into one group and work together to protect them. Pods of killer whales, or orcas, huntin groups, and working as a team helps animals like lions, wolves, and African hunting dogs make their kills.

BOTFLY INVASION

Botfly larvae are parasites. Human botfly larvae, for example, develop inside hosts such as people. However, the adults are big, noisy insects that would quickly be spotted. How do these flies get their young to hosts without being caught in the act? Botflies are sneaky. They catch female mosquitoes in midair and attach their eggs to them before letting them go. When a mosquito lands on a person to feed, the eggs quickly hatch, and the young burrow into the skin.

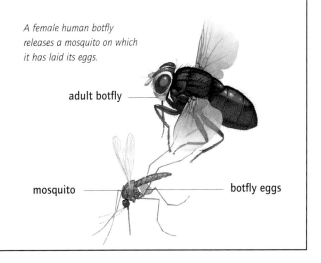

A female human botfly releases a mosquito on which it has laid its eggs.

adult botfly

mosquito

botfly eggs

HITCHING A RIDE

Many parasites use carriers called **vectors** to get around. Mosquitoes (see below) are the vectors for parasites that cause the deadly disease malaria. When a mosquito drinks blood, some of the parasites move into the insect. There they develop for a time before moving to the mosquito's salivary glands. The parasites are injected into a new host when the mosquito bites another person.

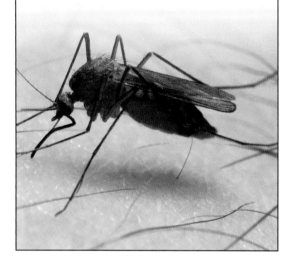

Animal societies

Some species have taken group living to the extreme. Animals such as corals, sponges, termites, and ants live in highly organized colonies where different individuals do different jobs. The Portuguese man-of-war lives in the open ocean. It looks like a jellyfish and uses stinging tentacles to capture prey. But a Portuguese man of-war is not one animal. It is a colony of hundreds of tiny individuals called **polyps**. The polyps come in different shapes and sizes depending on what function they carry out. A Portuguese man-of-war colony has a polyp filled with gas to give buoyancy, polyps with stings that form tentacles, and others that digest food. A fourth type of polyp in the colony produces offspring.

Social insects

Social insects—termites, ants, and some bees and wasps—also live in closely related groups. They are among the most successful animals on Earth. There are more species of ants in one square mile of Brazilian rain forest than there are species of primates on the entire planet.

Generally, only one individual in a social insect nest produces young. She is the queen. Other members of the colony called workers forage for food, tend to the young, or defend the nest. Bee, ant, and wasp workers are always female. Males are produced only at the end of the season to fertilize the next generation of queens.

Groups of insects with particular jobs are known as castes, and they may have an appearance suited to their role. Some soldier ants have massive mouthparts for fighting. Others have plug-shaped heads used to block entrances to the nest. Termite soldiers have nozzle-shaped heads used for spraying defensive chemicals at their enemies.

A Portuguese man-of-war is not one animal. It is a colony of separate polyps that carry out different functions such as killing prey, digesting food, and producing offspring.

Ants, such as these leaf cutter ants, live in colonies of thousands. They operate as highly organized groups.

Humans and other primates

Most animals other than social insects reproduce independently and can survive without belonging to a group. But many still associate with their own kind. Primates, the closest relatives of people, live in a range of social groups. Marmosets are monogamous (one male mates with only one female). They live in small family units in which both sexes look after the young. Mountain gorillas live in harems in which there is just one male to many females. One enormous male gorillla, called the silverback, provides the group of females with protection. In return he is allowed to mate with them and fathers all their young. This ensures that his genes are passed on to the next generation of gorillas.

Chimpanzees live in large troops of up to 80 individuals. Males and females may mate with several partners. Chimps from the same family tend to stick together within the group, but unrelated animals also form alliances. There are squabbles over food, mating, and grooming. Each animal has a social rank, which is crucial in deciding the outcome of disputes. Ancient human ancestors probably lived in societies similar to those of chimps. Later, they developed language to communicate complex information with other members of the group.

THOUGHTS AND MINDS

People have what scientists call a "theory of mind." This means people can appreciate that others have their own minds, thoughts, feelings, and perspectives on events. People can know when someone else is hungry or in pain or understand a different point of view. It also enables some to lie and trick others into doing what they want. Scientists argue over whether the theory of mind applies to other animals. Chimpanzees, dogs, dolphins, and parrots are all extremely intelligent animals, but do they have thoughts and emotions like people do? What do you think?

SCIENCE WORDS

- **commensalism** Relationship between organisms in which one benefits, and the other (the host) is unaffected.
- **mutualism** A relationship to the mutual benefit of two or more species.
- **polyp** Individual member of a colonial animal, such as coral or a siphonophore.
- **symbiosis** A relationship between different organisms.
- **vectors** An animal that carries a parasite between hosts.

COMMUNICATION

Communication is essential for fending off rivals, attracting a mate, warning others of danger, or showing them where to get food.

Animals are constantly communicating with each other. They have different reasons to communicate and different methods of communications too. Animals send out and receive signals using vision, touch, chemicals, and sound. Vision and touch are important at close quarters, while chemicals and sounds are more important over longer distances. Most animals use a combination of methods to communicate with each other.

Warding off rivals

Many animals hold territories to ensure food supplies or to attract a mate. They mark their territories against

Like humans, chimpanzees can communicate using facial expressions.

rivals using signals. Birds, for example, defend their territories with song. Boundaries can also be marked out with chemicals. Tigers mark points on boundaries with chemical-laden urine. The message is reinforced by visual signals such as scratches on trees.

Visual signals are often used to drive off rivals. These signals may take the form of displays. Honeypot ants, for example, scare away rival ants by walking stiffly on straight legs and making themselves look bigger.

The importance of badges

Visual signals can also be animals' physical features, or badges. Badges include the antlers of deer, the feathers of a peacock's tail, and the red bellies of

---

ELECTRIC CHATTER

Some animals are able to communicate in ways totally alien to people. Many fish, for example, can produce and detect electric fields. Electric eels (see below) use electric shocks to stun prey, but they also use their electric field to find their way around in dark river waters. Electric pulses are also used by these fish to communicate over short ranges with other electric eels.

The electric organs run along the body. They are composed of up to 200,000 electricity-producing disks. They can put out up to 500 volts—almost five times the voltage that comes from a wall socket.

INVITATION TO DINNER

Pheromones are not just used for mating but help many small animals form groups. Ticks feed on mammal blood. When a tick finds a good spot to feed, it releases a pheromone, and other ticks join it. The ticks release chemicals into the blood to keep it flowing and to stop it from clotting. More ticks mean more chemicals and less time spent feeding. This helps the ticks survive, since there is less chance of being discovered and removed by the host animal.

stickleback fish. These features are often a sign of dominance; dominant animals get more food and mates than other members of a group. Badges also indicate how good a mate an animal would be and help avoid fighting with other animals, which uses up energy and can sometimes lead to injury.

In Harris's sparrows, for example, dominance is related to the size of a black throat patch. Dominance can also depend on displays. A wolf holds its tail between its legs to indicate it is no threat to a dominant wolf with a higher-held tail. Dominance is important in social animals. Often only the dominant male and female will breed.

Long-distance calls

Visual communication is only useful at short range. To communicate over longer distances, many animals use chemicals called pheromones. Most male moths use their feathery antennae to detect pheromones released by the females. The chemicals invite the males to breed. A male sierra dome spider bundles a female's web into a ball as soon as he finds it. The web silk is rich with pheromones. By destroying the web, the male keeps other males from finding the female.

Sound is also important for long-distance contact. The calls of howler monkeys, for example, can be heard up to 3 miles (4.8 km) away! Howler monkeys use these sounds to protect their feeding ranges from other monkey groups.

Warning the family

For animals that live in groups with close relatives it pays to warn them of danger. An aphid under attack from a ladybug will release alarm pheromones.

GOOD VIBRATIONS

Sounds, in the form of vibrations, can travel a long way through the ground itself. In 2003, biologists found that elephants can tell if other elephants are in danger up to 10 miles (16 km) away. They can detect tiny tremors in the ground caused by the movement of distant herds. The elephants receive the sounds through their feet. Whales are able to communicate with others over long distances by **breaching**; they jump out of the water and slam themselves down again.

BEE DANCES

Honeybees tell others where to find food by dancing. The other bees collect information by touching the dancer. The round dance lets the bees know about nearby food sources. The longer the dance, the richer the food source. To pass on information about food sources more than 165 feet (50 m) from the hive, bees move in a different way. That is called the waggle dance.

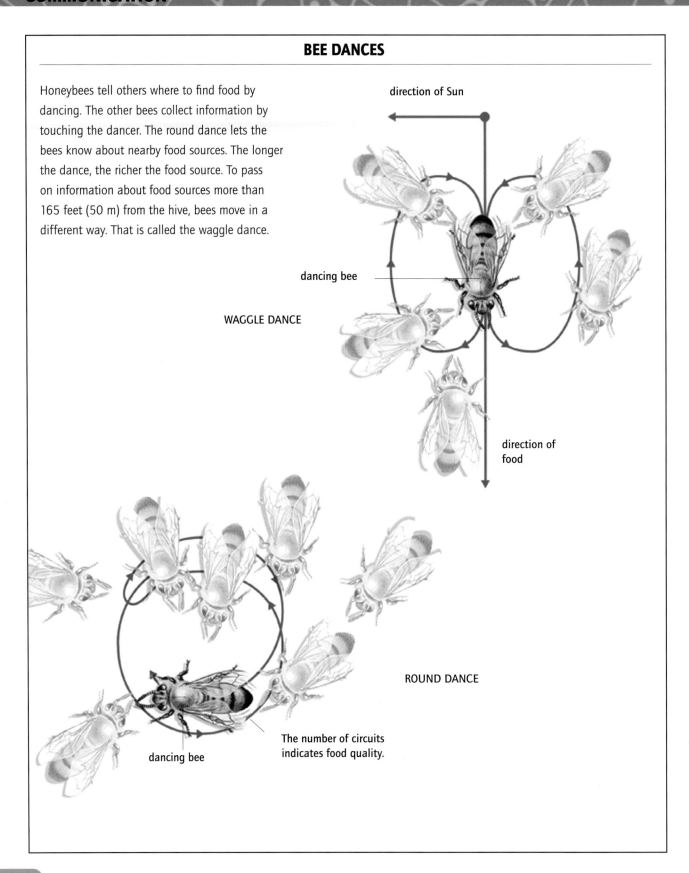

direction of Sun

dancing bee

WAGGLE DANCE

direction of food

ROUND DANCE

The number of circuits indicates food quality.

dancing bee

They alert all the nearby aphids so they can escape. Sound is also used to alert others quickly. A rabbit thumps its foot on the ground to warn others before taking cover, while beavers slap their tails on the water's surface.

Warning communication is at its most sophisticated in primates. Vervet monkeys, for example, use different alarm calls depending on the nature of the threat. A loud cough warns of a leopard, two coughs indicate an eagle, while a chutter sound is given when a snake gets near.

Calling other species

Animals regularly communicate with other species. Such communication usually acts as a warning to keep away, but sometimes communication helps both animals benefit. Honeyguides flash their white tail feathers at honey badgers to let them know they have found a beehive. The honey badger follows the bird to the hive. It breaks in with its strong claws to feast on the honey inside. The honeyguide eats the beeswax afterward. A relationship like this in which both partners benefit is called a mutualism.

Complex communications

Some animals are able to communicate very complex information. Honeybees can tell their nest mates where nectar-rich flowers are to be found. Dolphins

---

USING PHEROMONE TRAPS

Pheromones can sometimes be used to control pest animals. American freshwater crayfish were accidentally introduced to British waterways in the 1970s. American crayfish outcompeted the British crayfish for food and spread a disease that threatened to kill off their cousins. By setting up traps laced with the pheromones that American crayfish use to attract mates, scientists have been able to control the invaders.

---

can also communicate complex information, using a range of squeaks, peeps, and whistles. Dolphins even have signature whistles. These distinctive sounds are used for identification, just like a person's name. Other dolphins learn them so the animals can address each other as they communicate.

The most complex of all communication systems is human language. Very little is understood of how or when language appeared, but our ancestors could talk by around 200,000 years ago. Speech required dramatic changes to the structure of the tongue and larynx and to the brain, but it opened up a world of possibilities to ancient peoples. They could coordinate hunts and send complex, abstract information between groups or through the generations.

CHUCKLING CANINES

Next time you play with your dog, listen closely to the sounds it makes. In 2003 biologists discovered that when dogs are playing they laugh! The laughter sounds like panting to us, but it also contains low-frequency noises that people are unable to hear. These sounds communicate that the dogs are happy. Dog laughter is infectious too. Other dogs that hear it will try to join in the fun.

SCIENCE WORDS

- **breaching** When a whale leaps from the water and smashes its body down again to communicate with sound over long distances.
- **pheromone** Chemical released by an animal to attract, warn, or ward off others of the same species.

GLOSSARY

airfoil A surface that creates a force (lift) that allows animals to glide or fly.

alveolus Tiny air sac that forms bunches in the lungs through which exchange of oxygen and carbon dioxide takes place.

aorta Major artery leading directly from the heart.

asexual reproduction Production of young without the need for mating or the fusion of sex cells.

atrium One of a pair of heart chambers that receives blood before pumping it into a ventricle.

autonomic nervous system Part of the PNS that regulates the internal functions of the body automatically.

axial skeleton Part of the skeleton made up of the skull, backbone, and rib cage.

Batesian mimicry When a nonpoisonous animal looks like a poisonous species.

bile A yellow fluid secreted by the liver; in the intestine it helps in the emulsification and absorption of fats.

breaching When a whale leaps from the water and smashes its body down again to communicate with sound over long distances.

camouflage A pattern of coloration that allows an animal to blend in with its surroundings.

capillaries Tiny, thin-walled blood vessels through which oxygen and nutrients pass into cells, with waste going the other way.

carbohydrates Sugar molecules important in respiration.

carnivore Animal that catches other animals for food.

cellulose Chemical that forms tough molecules in the walls of plant cells.

central nervous system (CNS) The brain and spinal cord and their supporting cells.

cochlea Coiled structure in the inner ear that translates vibrations received at the tympanum into signals that go to the brain.

commensalism Relationship between organisms in which one benefits, and the other (the host) is unaffected.

courtship Display between a male and a female prior to mating.

detritivore Animal that feeds on dead animal or plant material.

diffusion The movement of molecules of liquids and gases from points of high concentration to points of lower concentration.

digestion The breakdown by enzymes of food into small, easily absorbed molecules in the stomach.

drag Force that opposes the movement of an object through water or air.

endocrine system System of glands that release hormones.

enzyme Protein that speeds up chemical reactions in organisms.

exoskeleton Tough outer skin of animals such as insects.

filter feeder Animal that sieves fine particles from water for food.

gait The way an animal moves.

gene Section of DNA that codes for the structure of a protein.

habitat The type of place in which an organism lives.

hemoglobin Pigment that occurs in red blood cells; binds to oxygen and carbon dioxide to carry these gases around the body.

herbivore Animal that feeds on plants.

hermaphrodite Animal with both male and female sexual organs.

hibernation To spend the winter in an inactive or dormant state.

honeydew Sugary fluid released by aphids.

hormone Chemical messenger that regulates life processes inside the body.

hydrostatic skeleton A fluid-filled structure used as a brace for muscles in many invertebrates.

hypothalamus Part of the brain that releases chemicals that control the pituitary gland.

invertebrate Animal that does not have a backbone.

larva The young of certain types of insects.

lek Place where males of certain species compete for mates.

lift Upward force produced by airflow over a wing.

migration Long-distance journey by animals such as birds to warmer places during winter weather.

mimicry Imitation of an object or another animal.

mineral An inorganic (non-carbon-containing) substance essential in tiny amounts for nutrition.

mobbing When small birds team up to drive away predators or egg thieves.

mucus Sticky fluid.

mutualism A relationship to the mutual benefit of two or more species.

nephron An excretory unit of the kidney.

neuron A nerve cell.

nocturnal Active at night.

omnivore Animal that eats both plant and animal matter.

ootheca Egg case of insects such as mantises.

osteoporosis A condition leading to brittle and fragile bones that mainly affects older women.

pepsin Enzyme in the stomach that breaks down proteins into polypeptides.

peripheral nervous system (PNS) A network of nerves that spreads from the central nervous system to the rest of the body.

peristalsis Waves of muscular contraction that ripple along the walls of the digestive system to keep food moving.

pheromone Chemical released by an animal to attract, warn, or ward off others of the same species.

pituitary gland Gland in the brain that releases hormones. They control the output of other endocrine glands.

placenta Organ that develops during pregnancy and supplies the growing young with food and oxygen, and takes away waste.

plankton Tiny animals, often the young of larger creatures, that float in the surface waters of the ocean.

platelet Tiny disk in the blood that helps clotting.

pleura One of a pair of delicate saclike membranes that wrap around the lungs.

polyp Individual member of a colonial animal, such as coral or a siphonophore.

prey Animal caught and eaten by another animal.

resilin Chemical with elastic properties that occurs in the skins of insects.

retina Sensitive layer of cells at the back of the eye that is stimulated by light.

sessile Animal that does not move during its adult life.

somatic nervous system Part of the PNS that gathers information from sensory organs and sends it to the central nervous system.

spermatophore A package containing sperm.

symbiosis A relationship between different organisms.

vector An animal that carries a parasite between hosts.

venom A poison delivered by a predatory animal to immobilize prey.

vertebrate Animal that has a backbone.

vortex A swirl of air that rolls from the wings of a flying or gliding animal.

FURTHER RESOURCES

PUBLICATIONS

Burnie, D. and Wilson, D. E. (eds). *Animal: The Definitive Guide to the World's Wildlife*. New York, UK: DK Publishing, 2001.

Gilpin, D. *History of Invention: Medicine*. New York: Facts on File, Inc., 2004.

Houston, R. *Parasites and Partners: Feeders*. Chicago, IL: Raintree, 2003.

Kalman, B. *What Are Camouflage and Mimicry?* New York: Crabtree, 2002.

Kim, M. and Gold, S. D. *The Endocrine and Reproductive Systems*. Berkeley Heights, NJ: Enslow Publishers, 2003.

Llewellyn, C. *The Big Book of Bones*. New York: Peter Bedrick Books, 1998.

Morgan, B. (ed). *Biomes Atlases*. Chicago, IL: Raintree, 2010.

Royston, A. *Why Do I Get a Toothache?: And Other Questions about Nerves*. Chicago, IL: Heinemann Library, 2003.

Tatham, B. *How Animals Communicate*. New York: Franklin Watts, Inc., 2004.

Viegas, J. *The Heart: Learning How Our Blood Circulates*. New York: Rosen Publishing Group, 2002.

Walker, R. *Body Science: How We Breathe*. North Mankato, MN: Smart Apple Media, 2004.

WEB SITES

Alien Empire
www.pbs.org/wnet/nature/alienempire/index.html
Learn about insects through interactive presentations, video clips, and games.

Biology in Motion
biologyinmotion.com
Interactive online activities and 3-D animations on body topics such as fat digestion, the thyroid gland, and the cardiovascular system.

BodyQuest
library.thinkquest.org/10348
Take a tour of the human body, with many graphics, experiments, and a quiz for each body system.

Brain Connection
www.brainconnection.com
A site with articles, brain-building activities, animations, library, gallery, and an anatomy section.

The Field Museum
www.fmnh.org/exhibits/online_exhib.htm
Chicago's museum of natural history has online exhibits about butterflies, lions, life underground, and dinosaurs.

Frogs
www.exploratorium.edu/frogs/index.html
Learn all about frogs at the San Francisco's Exploratorium feature.

The Heart Online
sln.fi.edu/biosci/index.html
Explore the heart and its development and structure. Follow blood through blood vessels, and learn how to have a healthy heart.

In Search of the Ways of Knowing Trail, Ituri Forest
www.brookfieldzoo.org/pagegen/wok/index_f4.html
Take a walk through the Ituri Forest in Central Africa and learn about plants, animals, and survival on the way.

Our editors have reviewed the Web sites that appear here to ensure that they are suitable for children and students. However, many Web sites frequently change or are removed, and we cannot guarantee that a site's future contents will continue to meet our high standards of quality. Be advised that children should be closely supervised whenever they access the Internet.

INDEX